I0619881

PRECIPICE

BY BRIAN MAYCOCK

SEVERED**PRESS**

PRECIPICE

CHAPTER 1

The man they had rescued was sitting next to Private Anthony Clarkson.

This was probably a bad idea.

Clarkson was addicted to eating fiery-hot chili peppers raw, and there was a running joke in their Special Forces unit that Clarkson's chili breath could stun a hog at twelve paces.

Harrow watched as Clarkson took one of the red devils out of his pocket, put it in his mouth and began to chew with relish.

The rescued man started to look horrified.

Harrow stifled a smile and looked away.

He had no idea who the man was. Need to know had not extended as far as the First Lieutenant on the ground. This was fine by him.

All he cared about was that the mission to rescue the man from the rebels' jungle compound had been a success and now they were going home.

As the vibrations of the helicopter carrying them there rattled his weary bones, Harrow closed his eyes and thought about what lay ahead.

His mood soured.

Harrow had joined the army as soon as he was old enough and everything he had achieved had been through sheer hard work and determination. His ambition had always been to make captain before his thirtieth birthday. He had not been planning on falling in love with the only daughter of a legendary Four-Star General along the way.

Sarah was pretty as a picture, wore her blond hair in a pony-tail, and had a smile that made Harrow go weak at the knees.

Joseph T. Masterton was a barrel-necked, square-jawed Titan of the military who sounded like he chewed gravel for breakfast. He had lost an eye in combat and refused to wear a patch, displaying the wound like yet another of the numerous medals he had been awarded.

Harrow had met the general once. It had not gone well.

While Sarah and her mother chatted in another room, Masterton had launched into an interrogation. It had soon become clear to Harrow that the general did not think Harrow was good enough for his little girl. There was no blue blood in Harrow's veins, no family fortune waiting in the wings.

The evening had ended with Masterton taking Harrow's hand in a vice-like grip and growling into his ear so that only Harrow could hear, "Stay away from my daughter."

Harrow had been furious. This was America in 2024 not England in the Victorian era. A father could not prevent a grown man and woman being together if that was what they wanted. So, a few weeks later, Harrow had followed his heart and proposed to Sarah, and she had said yes.

They had agreed to tell her parents about the engagement together. But her last message, sent just before he was deployed on this mission, gave him the idea that she was going to go ahead and break the news solo. If she had done this, there was going to be trouble brewing for Harrow.

Harrow felt the helicopter begin its descent and opened his eyes, back in the here and now.

The helicopter landed at their base and they disembarked. Their traumatized nameless package was delivered safely to a couple of anonymous-looking men wearing dark business suits who led him into an SUV with obscured windows.

As the SUV sped away and the unit watched the exhaust fumes hanging for a moment in the stifling desert air, Clarkson asked, "Where's our hero's welcome?"

That brought a ripple of jaded laughs, then everyone started to troop towards the hut where they would dump their weapons.

Harrow noticed the two MPs loitering near the hut but did not pay any real attention to them. There were dozens of military personnel of all types going about their business that he could see, and a thousand more on the base overall.

In contrast to Harrow's ragged appearance after long days and nights in the jungle, the MPs' uniforms were crisply clean and their chins freshly scraped.

And, all of a sudden, they were turning towards

him, taking a step closer.

One of them looked Harrow in the eye and said, "We need you to come with us."

There was no 'Sir' or a salute.

Harrow had been around long enough to know there was no point in arguing with them. He'd find out what the problem was soon enough, and was confident it could be easily sorted out.

He went quietly as they escorted him to a windowless building. The room they took him to inside was furnished with a concrete slab in place of seats and a filthy metal toilet in one corner.

Harrow took this in, then span around to face the MPs. He had to speak out now.

"You can't just put me in a cell like this," he protested. "I have rights..."

The door slamming in his face and the sound of a lock turning ended his protests. In a flash of anger, Harrow kicked out at the door, then went over to the concrete block and sat down.

He did not have to wait long before the lock clicked loudly and the door swung back open. A captain stepped into the cell and hovered by the door as it was closed behind him.

"First Lieutenant Thomas Harrow?" he asked, sounding bored.

"Yes," Harrow snapped back. "What the hell is going on?"

If the captain gave a damn, it was still impossible to tell as he replied, "While you were on deployment, your locker was searched following information received. Two antiquities were discovered. Small, priceless objects that were looted from a museum in the Middle East when you were on a peace-keeping mission there three months ago. As a result of this you are going to now be taken before the Commanding Officer of the base and charged with theft and numerous other offences. I have been assigned to be your lawyer and I will be straight with you, Harrow, there is not a thing I can do. This is an open and shut case. I take it you are familiar with that phrase?"

Harrow's blood was boiling. He shot to his feet and said, "I know bullshit when I hear it."

Righteous anger, but the a-hole captain still did not care. He knocked on the door and said in the same monotone voice, "Open up, guards. You might want to have your batons ready. This individual's attitude is as unpleasant as his odor."

"You son of a bitch," Harrow muttered as two new MPs – who looked like they could have done with spending more time evolving and less time working out in the gym – entered the cell.

Harrow's fury was unabated, but all he was going to get by lashing out was a beating, so he held his hands up in mock surrender and said, "Let's get this over with and then I am going to find myself a proper lawyer."

With an MP on either side, he was marched out of the cell. It did not take long for them to reach the

Commander's office. Before they went inside, another man was bundled out through the door by two more stone-faced escorts.

He was short and wiry and, seeing Harrow and his unwanted entourage, flashed a smile Harrow's way and said brightly, "Lovely day for a stroll in the sun. My friends call me JJ. You need anything getting, you just let me know."

Harrow stared at the man as he was escorted away. That was one screwed up individual.

Harrow did not have time to worry about other people, though. He had a whole heap of problems of his own.

Now the way was clear, he was pushed unceremoniously forwards, and soon found himself standing to attention before the Commander, who started to repeat the outrageous allegations.

As the lies went on, Harrow had a sudden revelation. There was only one explanation that made any sense.

It was the general. He had set Harrow up to stop the marriage.

CHAPTER 2

Harrow was not going to make it to captain before his thirtieth birthday.

His claims of a conspiracy instigated by a hugely respected general had fallen on deaf ears and, after twelve months in military prison, he had been dishonorably discharged from the army.

Disembarking from the bus which had taken him from the base to the nearest city, he only had one thing on his mind that did not involve disemboweling people in uniform.

First, he had to get online. His personal phone had been seized by the MPs as part of their bogus investigation and they had not returned it. So, he bought a cheap burner phone with data from a drug store and did a search for Sarah on social media.

He could not remember her phone number but hoped he would be able to contact her this way. He would send a message to tell her that he was innocent and that he still loved her. When he did, it was going to be okay. It was not going to be a cakewalk, but love would find a way.

He found a number of Sarah Mastertons before he clicked on a page that was hers. Because he was a virtual stranger on this device, access was limited and there was no option to DM her.

But that was not the problem.

The problem was the photograph, which all users could see displayed prominently at the top of the page. It showed Sarah in a white wedding dress standing next to a man in full dress military uniform. Sarah's smile was dazzling.

Harrow blinked, barely able to believe what he was seeing.

But there was no question about it. The woman he loved with every fiber of his being had ditched him and moved on big style.

Harrow did not recognize the scum she had hooked up with, but assumed he came from a wealthy family and had probably graduated top of his class at West Point thanks to some serious greasing of the pole.

Harrow hated this stranger more than anyone he had ever hated before.

And he hated Sarah. He hated the whole damn world.

He swore and threw the phone to the ground, breaking it. Only it was not broken enough. Not by a long way. He brought the heel of his boot down onto the lousy, stinking piece of junk and ground it into fragments.

He called it every name under the sun while he did, then looked up, his chest heaving, his face coated with sweat.

He got the feeling that most of the passers-by who had stopped and were making calls on their own phones while they eyed him warily had just dialed 911.

"Screw the lot of you," he shouted at the top of his voice and went in search of a drink.

The area around the back of the bus station was run-down and well served by seedy-looking bars. He chose one that had all its windows boarded up with plywood, stepped over the cigarette butts piled up in front of the door and headed on in.

There was a song playing on the jukebox about love gone wrong, sawdust on the floor and the smell of stale beer and sweat in the air. It was the pits.

As long as he could get a shot of bourbon, Harrow did not care. After his first drink he was going to have another, then another. Sometimes, getting oblivious was all a man had left.

Harrow walked over to the bar, lowered himself onto a stool, put down a bill and told the barman, "Glass of your finest gut-rot."

The drink he was handed was fierce. It burnt all the way down and left Harrow gasping.

"Another," he said hoarsely.

While he was waiting to be served, Harrow realized someone was looking at him – a short, wiry stranger with gelled-back hair who was propping up the bar half a dozen stools down.

He wore jeans, a t-shirt and leather jacket, and what was either cologne or insect repellent. There was a gold chain around his neck, and a watch on his wrist that would have been worth a couple of grand if it was genuine.

It made no difference to Harrow if it was or not. He ignored the stranger and turned his attention to the drink being placed on the bar in front of him. The glass it was in looked like it had not been cleaned since the turn of the century, but he wasn't worried about germs. Nothing could survive in the booze he was about to drink in one.

He raised the glass to his lips and was about to tip it into his mouth when the stranger said, "I know you. You're Lieutenant Harrow."

Harrow lowered the glass. If he had wanted a conversation he would have gone somewhere with natural light and ventilation.

What he wanted to do was to get blind drunk in peace, and this asshole was disturbing him.

He swiveled round and snarled, "Go to hell."

Which made the stranger grin. "Not this time of year," he replied cheerfully. "It's way too hot." Then he added, "My friends call me JJ. I can tell you don't remember me but I recall you. After I saw you being taken in to see the Commander, I asked around. Heard you were an officer and gentleman by the name of Harrow. Collecting and storing information that might be useful to my future business ventures is all part of my approach, you see."

Harrow was even less impressed than he had been and made this clear: "You'll be approaching the exit with my boot mark on your backside if you don't shut your mouth and leave me be."

By now, he'd also remembered seeing the man, JJ, on the base – briefly that one time outside the Commander's office, and maybe a couple more times among the other prisoners in the exercise yard.

The man was ex-military, present day jerk, and not taking clear advice to back off.

He was moving to the stool next to Harrow instead, holding up two fingers in the direction of the barman and saying, "A couple of bourbons, neat, the legal stuff. My body is a temple not a garbage dump. Hand one to my friend here."

"I am not your friend and I do not want your drink," Harrow insisted.

JJ did not give up.

"Well," he murmured, "How about a job then? Doing what you do best, soldiering."

Harrow's shoulders slumped. "I'm no soldier anymore." His words were tinged with sadness.

JJ downed his drink in one thirsty gulp, shuddered as it hit his system, and sounded like his vocal chords had been scorched when he went on, "Not officially no, but they can't take away the skills you learnt and the instincts you developed. You will be a fighter till the day you die, Lieutenant Harrow, so go with the flow and earn some good money while you're at it. I've put together a crew of former soldiers and we've got our first assignment. There is a plane waiting at an airstrip nearby and we will be seeing action by tomorrow first light. What do you say?"

Harrow shook his head and pushed the fresh glass of booze away. "It's not for me."

JJ shrugged. It seemed his pitch was over. He drained the second glass himself and set off walking for the door.

"Good riddance," Harrow said under his breath, then, unbidden, the image of Sarah's smile in the wedding photograph came back to him. It was the smile of someone who was truly happy.

Harrow put his head in his hands. He could never be happy without her.

Which left him with what?

He could stay where he was. Have more lousy drinks in this filthy bar followed by a night in a motel room if he had any money left.

Or, he could go fight as a mercenary in some distant, dangerous place and let loose every ounce of rage he was feeling.

He looked up and yelled out, "Wait!" then hurried through the door and back out onto the street, where JJ was waiting for him in a car. The engine was running. It sounded sick. The rest of the car looked like scrap metal in waiting. But JJ had his arm draped out the open window and a relaxed smile on his face as if he was chilling in a cool, classic set of wheels.

He opened the passenger door and said with a drawl that had not been there before, "Let's roll, Lieutenant. Our future awaits us."

Harrow did not know whether to laugh or cry as he got into the car and they sped away.

It was not a smooth ride. Every rut in the road sent shock waves through Harrow's spine.

When they left the tarmac and drove through an open gate in a wire mesh fence onto grass that cushioned the wheels, he felt a degree of relief. This lasted all of a minute, then he saw the plane they were heading towards.

It was parked up on the edge of a narrow runway that had weeds sprouting from cracks in its surface. Two old-school propellers were attached to the wings on each side of a rust-riddled fuselage.

As they came closer, Harrow could see holes in the metal where the rust had eaten through. The rubber on the wheels extended below the plane was worn away as well.

The bare rims glinted in the sunlight as Harrow's ride pulled up alongside. JJ hopped out and hurried over towards five men who were loitering on the other side of the plane.

Wondering if a few more drinks followed by a night with bed bugs and cockroaches for company in a no-star motel would have been better after all, Harrow followed.

JJ was working his way along the group exchanging high-fives, until he got to the last man, who Harrow saw was at least six-feet-nine tall.

JJ would have needed a step-ladder to high-five this man. They fist bumped instead. Harrow noticed the man had what looked like home-made tattoos on his knuckles. The kind that a soldier on active duty would not have been allowed to get. If they were serving a sentence in a military prison however...

JJ interrupted Harrow's chain of thought by calling out, "Hey, Lieutenant, come and meet the squad."

Harrow said what was on his mind: "That's a mighty small squad."

JJ did not bat an eyelid. "Quality over quantity. You want brute force, hire wrestlers or doormen. You want elite, you employ JJ, Lieutenant Tom Harrow, the Pastor, Salgado Joe and the Banjo twins."

Apart from really not liking being included in that dubious sounding list, Harrow also noted there was one short in the name check.

Without being asked, JJ filled in the gap. "And that there is Billy," he said, pointing at a man who was drawing in smoke from a skinny cigarette that Harrow assumed contained hardly any tobacco. "Billy's our pilot on this fine day."

Harrow's heart sank another notch. He glanced back at the junk-pile car. The keys were still in the ignition. He could just take it and drive back to town. The bar would still be open. Bars like that never closed.

That was the only intelligent thing to do. This was a freak show, not a military force.

He was only half paying attention when JJ

added, "Course, we are still waiting on Fast Eddie. From the sounds of it, this is likely him now."

Harrow listened but all he could hear was the sound of sirens. They were distant, but coming closer.

He raised a hand over his eyes to try and shield them from the glare of the sun and made out a car speeding towards them. A trail of dust was being thrown up into the air behind it as it left the road and began to careen across the grass.

It screeched to a halt a few feet away from JJ's car and a man jumped out. The others seemed to be taking his arrival as their cue to board the plane. Backpacks were being thrown inside, followed by the band of men. The pilot took another draw on the glowing stub left in his fingers then tossed it aside and moved languidly towards the cockpit.

"Forget this," Harrow said to himself and turned to head towards JJ's car – just as the police cruisers came screaming into view.

There were three cop cars, each with a two-man crew, and as the cruisers screeched to a halt the police officers jumped out, their weapons raised.

If any of them shouted a warning, Harrow did not hear it before the bullets started to fly.

Harrow was left with no choice. He sprinted towards the plane. Its engines were gunning into life and it was starting to roll unevenly along the runway, its exposed rims screeching like harpies.

Harrow felt the air by his ear ripple as a bullet

missed him by a fraction.

The plane was picking up speed now. Its side door was still open and the big man was holding out a hand in Harrow's direction.

It had been a long time since Harrow had believed in a higher being. Dumb chance was the best on offer as he leapt and grabbed for the man's hand.

The next thing he knew he was being dragged inside. He twisted round, saw the ground behind him falling away and a rabble of cops all firing at once.

Then his boots were through the door, which was slammed shut. A bullet cracked the glass, the engine roared, turbulence grabbed the plane and shook it violently, and Harrow was left sitting on the floor with his mouth hanging open.

There was no going back now.

CHAPTER 3

Over the last few hours Harrow had lost count of the number of times the engine had cut out and they had begun to hurtle downwards only for Billy to pull them back from the brink. They did not have far to fall before catastrophe struck either. Flying this low was a sure sign to Harrow that they were trying to evade civilian radar systems.

Being on high-stakes assignments back when he was in the military had felt much better than this. For all the risks, at least then he knew he was part of an efficient, experienced organization.

Here, he was in deep with a bunch of snoring, grunting, scratching, belching curs. Aside from the sheen of smoothness JJ sported, they wore a ragtag mix of torn, stained combat gear, denim and cracked leather. Holsters for pistols and knives hung from belts, and through a broken zip in one of the backpacks Harrow could see a number of rifles. There was nothing that looked under ten years old, nothing bought legally either he assumed.

So whatever job JJ had lined up for them, at least they were not going in buck naked when it came to arms.

But a gun that jammed or misfired at the wrong moment was about as much use as a baseball bat in a fire fight. Though at least a baseball bat could not give you third degree burns or blow your fingers off. Harrow scratched his stubble and wondered if one of these good old boys would have a slugger in their kit. If they had, he would claim it and keep it close. Maybe use it to crack a few skulls.

It had grown dark outside and when Harrow grinned at this prospect, he could see his reflection smiling back in the small window opposite where he sat.

He once more wanted to fight above all else. He wanted to unleash the anger that had been building inside him since his arrest. He dearly hoped he would get the chance to do that when they arrived at their destination. If they arrived.

The engine had cut out again and the plane was falling. Harrow closed his eyes, gritted his teeth. The engine spluttered, made a sharp banging sound over and over. It sounded like a death rattle.

He felt the plane going into a nose dive. It started to spiral. God-damn oversized tin can. The only thing that was going to be unleashed was his guts and gore when the plane crashed and he was spread over the ground.

Then the rattle stabilized. He could hear a steady drone and they were slowly levelling out, and ascending.

Harrow breathed out, opened his eyes. On one side of him the big man was snoring. Next to him JJ was talking in his sleep about profit margins. The others had slept through their latest close call as well.

It was just him and Billy who were awake.

"How much longer till we get there?" Harrow called out to the pilot.

"I'd say we're just about at our destination," Billy yelled back.

Harrow twisted his neck to try and see where they were heading, but there was only darkness below.

Then Billy hollered, "Just need for them to light the fires and we can begin our descent."

And Harrow understood.

On the ground, the first flickers of a flame became visible. A single light in the dark, until a second flame appeared two dozen feet along, then another. A third fire directly opposite this was the next to break through the darkness.

In the space of a few minutes two crude lines marked out by fires had created a landing strip.

The plane had overflown this by now, but it banked and was soon dipping towards the ground. It was going to land dead central between the fires.

Harrow had to admit he was impressed. Then he remembered the wheels, the lack of rubber, and braced himself.

The plane bounced once – and with enough force to actually wake the big man from his slumber – before landing with a resounding thud and grinding to a sudden halt.

Harrow's head was jerked back. He rubbed his

neck and groaned. He probably had whiplash. Well, he'd just have to deal with it. They were on the ground and Harrow was ready to roll.

The rest of the dozing men were stirring. Not leaping into action, but yawning and stretching and breaking wind.

JJ got to his feet, rubbed his hands together and said, "Right, here's the score. Our client is General Xavier Rodrigues. He's a big cheese here south of the border and is going to throw his hat into the ring for the next presidential elections. But before then he needs to get some local competition off his back. They're real hard-ass dudes, who are threatening the compound where he's based, and we're here to take them out of the picture. Everyone cool with that?"

JJ did not wait for any answers before nodding in Harrow's direction. "Lieutenant Harrow is going to be in charge while the bullets are flying and the bad guys are dropping like flies."

That was news to Harrow, but it made its own sense. JJ was a fast-talking chancer but if he had ever been in combat, let alone led... well, Harrow had serious doubts about that. He pictured JJ behind the front line selling everything he could find that was not nailed down.

"That's fine by me," Harrow said. "With one condition. When the fighting starts, no one gets in the way between me and the enemy. We clear on that?"

There was grunting and nodding then they

started to haul their gear off the plane.

Harrow had not been introduced to this gallery of deadbeats yet, but he was figuring out who was who.

Two of the men were identical all the way up to their blond buzz cuts. The Banjo twins were also both using bayonets as tooth picks.

He already knew who Fast Eddie was. The man who'd had the law on his tail was slotting a magazine into a semi-automatic. His short dark hair had a ruler-straight parting, his goatee was trimmed neatly, and he had a single blood-red star tattooed under his right eye. A distinctive feature probably plastered over most-wanted galleries in a number of states.

As for the last two... Harrow saw one of them was taking sticks of dynamite out of a backpack and tucking them into the pockets of a padded waistcoat. Then looking to the sky, clasping his hands together and crying out, "For what we are about to obliterate may we be truly grateful. A-men!"

Harrow hoped the explosives were not as unstable as the Pastor appeared to be.

Which just left Salgado Joe.

If his names had been reversed, Harrow would have assumed the big man was on a visit back home, Salgado being a common surname in South America.

As it was, Harrow was intrigued enough to wander up to the big man and ask, "Why do they call you Salgado Joe?"

The big man was no oil painting. His nose looked to have been broken multiple times and there was a dent in his shaven skull. He smiled at Harrow's question, showing two rows of badly capped teeth, before he answered, "Because I am exotic, Lieutenant Harrow. According to the lady as gave me the name."

Harrow wished he hadn't asked, and when JJ waved him and the others over to a pair of jeeps parked up beyond the now weakening flames, he was happy to head over.

Billy was over by the jeeps as well, smoking a slim cigarette and looking chilled out. "I'll see you guys when you get back," he said and patted Harrow on the shoulder.

Leaving Billy in a cloud of smoke, they drove off towards the sun just rising over the horizon.

The sky was streaked with scarlet and it gave the scrubland they were driving through an aura of beauty it did not deserve.

Dust from the track they were speeding along spat up from under the wheels. The fronds of trees which looked riddled with disease hung low on either side of them. Occasionally there was a break in the foliage where a shack had sprung up. Toothless old men and women crouched on porches could have been propped up corpses for all the interest they showed in the jeeps crowded with vagabond soldiers all brandishing weapons. A three-legged dog in the doorway of one of the shacks was the only thing that seemed bothered by their presence and yapped frantically in their wake.

After about an hour on the track, Harrow's eyes were stinging with the dust that had come his way. He blinked rapidly to try and clear them out, and when he tried looking again could see dark smoke spiraling up into the sky, then moments later the high stone walls of a compound directly ahead.

Whatever was on fire was beyond that wall.

Harrow's guts tightened as the jeeps picked up speed.

CHAPTER 4

There were no guards on the compound's gates. No welcoming committee. Just a scene of utter devastation.

Inside its walls, the compound was laid out like a small town. The now charred, smoking remains of its wooden buildings stretched out as far as the eye could see. Between the wreckage, bodies lay strewn everywhere. Blood, already dried hard in the intensifying sun, caked the ground around each corpse.

Harrow and JJ stood in an open square looking up at a flag pole.

"Did you meet the general?" Harrow asked.

"Not in person. We talked over a video link." JJ ran his hand through his hair and gulped before adding, "But I still recognize him."

He lowered his gaze, spat into the dirt.

The uniformed figure hanging by a noose from the top of the flag pole spun gently in a breeze that Harrow wished he'd been able to feel on his skin.

It was hotter than hell and the stench of death was all pervading.

Harrow clenched his fists. They had got there too late, after the general's enemies had made their move. After the fighting had finished. The anger he held inside continued to build.

But he wasn't a monster.

"Fan out," he ordered, "See if there are any survivors, and if there are we help them the best we can."

JJ was sitting on the ground looking distraught. Probably thinking about the fee that he was not going to collect. The others were standing around, looking surly.

"Now," Harrow growled and they drifted off slowly.

A few minutes later, Fast Eddie was the first to reappear. "Got a live one," he told Harrow and JJ. "Over this way."

They followed him as he weaved his way through the carnage until they reached the shell of a building. Inside what was left of the walls, metal bars were fixed over an opening in the floor.

Harrow flicked on a flashlight, directed the beam through the opening, and saw a man crouched in a corner of a pit.

Harrow figured they had stumbled across some kind of dungeon, and one from which there was no parole from the way the bars looked fixed permanently in place with no locks in sight. On the bright side, being down there must have also saved the man's life when the compound was attacked.

JJ started to turn away. "Dude's a loser. I say we leave him, and get out of here. This whole place is a waste of time and there isn't a cent to be made."

Harrow wasn't having that. "I'm not leaving him

here to die. Fast Eddie, go fetch the Pastor, tell him we need his dynamite."

When the Pastor got there, Harrow pointed at the bars and asked, "Can you blast those loose without making the whole floor collapse?"

A smile that Harrow did not like crossed the Pastor's face before he replied, "I can move mountains and wipe heathens from the face of the earth. Little thing like this, be a cinch."

Harrow noticed JJ and Fast Eddie were already backing away. Salgado Joe and the Banjo twins were out there as well, no doubt wanting to see what was going on.

Harrow paid them no heed. He leant over the bars and told the prisoner, "Cover your head. We're going to get you out of there with a dose of TNT."

Harrow paced out what he hoped was a safe distance and waited for the explosion.

It came moments later, a loud 'thud' which was followed by a shower of dirt cascading out into the open. Then the Pastor emerged. He looked extremely pleased with himself.

The man that limped out after him was shielding his face from the sunlight. He was painfully thin and his skin was sallow and deeply lined. Tears ran down his grizzled face.

"Thank you for freeing me," he said quietly, his voice trembling with emotion.

JJ was not interested. He glared at Harrow. "Come on! You've done your good deed, now let's make tracks and find a way to make some serious money."

Harrow's attention was still on the prisoner.

He was rubbing his eyes and looking around at his rescuers.

Harrow saw a spark of life in the man's gaze, and heard a strength in his voice that had not been there before when the man spoke up.

"I wouldn't be so hasty. I can tell you how you can get money. The kind of money that will make you rich beyond your wildest dreams."

JJ looked like he was about laugh this off, but held himself back. Harrow could almost see the cogs turning. A good businessman never turned down an opportunity – or was that simply good old-fashioned greed Harrow now noticed on JJ's face?

"Go on," JJ said.

The man stood a little taller, a little prouder, and began to speak.

"My name is Max Cortez. I grew up in a shanty town with a belly swollen by hunger. My family were farmers who spent their short lives scrabbling in the dirt. But I knew as soon as I could think for myself that I was not going to be like them and I began running with a gang of thieves. It was the greatest time of my life. I had cash to burn and a pretty girl in every village we passed through."

He started to leer and laugh at this memory, a laugh that turned into a hacking cough. He got control of himself, hawked out a fat, disgusting yellow globule of phlegm, then went on.

"It was the summer of 1974 and I had just turned twenty-one when the gang raided the vaults of a bank and stole hundreds of gold coins. We stuffed saddlebags with our haul and galloped away on our steeds. A single one of those coins would have made a man a king in the town where I grew up. With all of them, the world would bend its knee before us. We could have had anything. But it was not to be."

He sighed, wiped the back of his hand across his mouth.

"The cops were on our trail and it looked hopeless. They were going to track us down like dogs and justice would have been dispensed out in the open with a bullet to our heads. We were close to a river and the leader of the gang made a desperate decision. They would dismount and carry the sacks of coins over their shoulders as they swan across the river. Because I was the youngest, I was to stay behind with the horses and lead them off to create a false trail. I stood and watched helplessly then as my brothers began to wade into the water. But it was a mistake. The water caught them in its embrace and swept them away. I heard their screams cut short as they were carried through the rapids and towards a vast precipice. They hurtled to their deaths over the edge of the precipice, taking the coins with them. I was devastated but all I could do was try to save myself. I set the false trail and managed to escape. I alone carried the secret with me of the fate of my brothers and the haul, but I could not act on it. I turned to petty thievery to survive and made the most stupid mistake of my life by stealing from the general. He had me thrown into that pit, where I festered year after year, until I had given up hope that I would ever see the light of day again and have the chance to retrieve the coins. Well, I was wrong. Destiny has brought me seven noble heroes."

Saying this, he bowed to them. Then winced, and when he straightened up, held the small of his back. Harrow pictured worn joints creaking.

He could not imagine why Max would spin them a tale, but he did have one question.

JJ beat him to it, asking, "What's the deal?"

Max's eyes were watering again, but this time from the pain in his spine. He wiped them and said, "Imprisonment has broken me, but if you can get the coins, all I ask is to keep a handful so I can afford tequila and fine food and to spend my few remaining nights on this earth in the arms of a beautiful woman. And with perhaps a little left over for a fine tombstone after I die with a smile on my face."

Max showed the cracked, yellowed teeth he would be displaying in his grave as he waited for their answer.

He did not have long to wait.

JJ said, "Deal. Now show us the way."

Max showed more of his trashed teeth.

This was on.

Harrow looked around for the general's last surviving men – the pair who'd lit the flames for the makeshift landing strip then driven them here.

He saw them weeping over the bodies of their comrades.

"Leave them to it," JJ said by his side.

This time Harrow did not argue. The general's men could take their chances and, without being asked, the Banjo twins were jumping in behind the steering wheels, starting the engines.

The rest of them all leapt on board. Well, apart from Max, who was strictly slow motion in everything he did after his years of incarceration. And then they were off - racing over open ground.

Max, in the lead jeep with JJ, stabbed a finger in the air and they veered off in that direction.

Harrow in the following jeep spat out gritty dirt thrown up by the wheels. Abandoned shacks collapsing in on themselves rushed past. The shell of a car propped up on bricks was out front of one. Harrow saw the head of a snake flickering inside, and then it was gone, left behind.

The Banjo twin driving Harrow's jeep had a manic grin on his face.

Harrow felt the same. Adrenaline rushed through his veins as they rushed on.

Two crazed hours later, Harrow saw Max shout in JJ's ear. JJ's arm shot up and both jeeps screeched to a halt.

Harrow jumped out and ran towards the sound of running water. He scrambled up a bank, and the river was there.

It was fast moving, but not that wide, not that deep. It would have come up to Harrow's shoulders if he'd tried wading through. He could see why the gang would have attempted to lose their pursuers here.

He moved closer to the water's edge, peered through the clear water. The rocks on the riverbed were worn smooth. They'd be perilous as hell underfoot.

One wrong step and you'd be losing balance, caught in the current.

He looked up, followed the course of the river to his left, and shivered despite the brutal heat of the day.

You'd be caught and carried helplessly into the rapids and smashed against the rocks that jutted out from the swirling, dervish dance that the water had become.

Then hurtle over the edge of the precipice.

Be lost to sight.

Harrow imagined Max watching all those years before as his gang of criminal brothers fell to their deaths.

He turned around and saw Max sitting on the ground slumped against one of the jeeps.

He looked beat. The drive can't have been easy after all the years of only being able to pace up and down in a pit. Being back here must have been dredging up hideous memories as well.

Harrow felt for him and strode over, grabbed a bottle of water and an energy bar and held them out to Max.

He wiped a hand shakily across his brow as he shook his head. "Thank you, friend, but clean water and fancy candy would be too much for my guts. I'll stick to what I got used to in the pit."

Saying this, he flipped over a flat stone lying on the ground near his feet, exposing a fat, pale, wriggling grub. Max picked it up, popped it in his mouth whole and began to chew contentedly.

Harrow opened the water himself and took a sip. He put the energy bar back, his own appetite gone, then said, "Max, you stay here and keep an eye on the jeeps. The rest of you, we'll be travelling light, so grab only what you need to survive and leave everything else here."

They got to it. Coming straight from the dive-bar, Harrow had brought nothing, so the others shared kit with him, including a rifle that was still in decent nick and a hunting knife.

His mind went back to the flight and he said jokingly, "Anyone got a baseball bat?"

There were shrugs, smiles, but, no one had.

Harrow smiled himself. It had been worth asking. And now it was time to move off.

They followed the edge of the land as it arced around to one side of the precipice. After twenty minutes, they could look back and see the precipice side on. It was vast and from the angle they were peering at it seemed to run on forever.

They had no idea where the base was.

But that was where they needed to be to begin their search for the gold coins.

"This is insane," Fast Eddie muttered as he stared over the edge.

"Yeah," Salgado Joe said. "I mean I want to be filthy stinking rich as much as the next man, but this is batshit crazy, no other way to put it."

"Sure, it is crazy," JJ replied. "But is it crazier than being in the army and risking your neck for a basic wage and three square-meals a day, or working nine-to-five on civvy street and spending forty years bored to tears. At least this kind of crazy might see us walk away as winners."

He said that last part real quiet, and the others just looked at each other.

Then Salgado Joe said, "You put it like that, then, yeah, I'm in."

"How about the rest of you?" JJ asked. "No one is being forced into this. You can stay here with Max and there's no shame in that. Hell, when we've found the haul, I'll even pass on a gold coin or two to help see you on your way 'fore we fly back to the States. But aside from that, and the cut we've agreed with Max, the lion's share goes to those who go on the mission and risk their necks."

Fast Eddie said, "Count me in."

The Pastor nodded in agreement.

The Banjo twins both held a thumb up.

Salgado Joe grunted, "Why not."

Harrow had never wavered. He wanted to be wealthy, sure. He wanted a fight more. He set off walking and the others fell into step behind him.

To their left scrubland stretched out, to their right there was a sheer drop. Even with hard-core climbing gear, it would have been a dance with death to try and head down.

So, they scrambled on. The line they followed continued its slow curve and the precipice grew smaller in the view behind them.

Harrow had no problem with that. He had his bearings and knew he could find his way back towards where the base must wait.

They just needed to find a way down.

It continued to evade them until the sun was low in the sky and Harrow noticed a possible path. A narrow strip of land that wound down. The gradient was extreme and one slip and they'd go tumbling down, breaking ankles, breaking necks.

It was a hell of a gamble.

One they would take.

Harrow took a deep breath and began to descend.

CHAPTER 5

Six days of struggling down vicious slopes, skin shredded by gripping gaps barely there to cling on, nerves shredded by rocks constantly falling away beneath their feet.

Six nights of fractured sleep camped out on narrow ledges, knowing one roll over the wrong way and that was it.

Oh, and the fire ants they dislodged when their nest joined rocks sent flying. Those bastards bit.

Plus, there was Salgado Joe's bout of explosive diarrhea. They'd had to wait for hours while he squatted with his backside over yet another ledge. There are some sights no man should see, so they looked away. Some sounds no man should have to ever listen to, but there was no way not to.

Being a soldier had been an ordeal for all of them.

Being dogs of war turned treasure hunters truly sucked so far.

It was bad, the descent.

Then, on the seventh morning they were thrown a new curve ball.

An unbroken line of dense jungle stood in their path.

Harrow drove on straight for it, dragging the others in his wake.

He followed the slope down towards the jungle's edge, and was pleased to see the nearest thing they'd had to a break in far too long. The ground seemed to be levelling out.

His muscles were screaming at him to stop, had been constantly for day after day, but he increased his pace. But, before he'd gone far into the undergrowth, he found himself being overtaken. Salgado Joe brandished two machetes as he moved purposely into the lead.

Thanks to his bulk, he moved through the jungle like a wrecking ball. With added blades.

Harrow kept pace a few feet behind. The Banjo twins, the Pastor, and Fast Eddie followed, with JJ at the rear.

As they made their way deeper and deeper into the jungle, Harrow navigated using the glimpses of the sun he could catch through the thick canopy and by noting the side of the trees moss grew on when his view was cut off.

Though they'd lost sight of the precipice on the second day of the descent, he was still confident they were on the right track. Any niggles, he pushed aside. Now was a time to trust himself because doubt would slow them down.

Every now and then he put a hand on Salgado Joe's elbow – his shoulder was a strain to reach – and asked the big man to deviate to the left or the right.

Each time, Salgado Joe would turn round and

nod to show he understood. His bald head dripped with sweat and more sweat pooled in the dent in his skull before sloshing out when he nodded.

Insects dislodged from branches and vines were stuck to his flesh by the sweat as well.

It would have been an all you could eat buffet for Max.

Harrow hadn't wasted any energy worrying if Max would be okay. He was out of that hideous pit, a free man with everything he needed to survive all around him.

He remained focused on putting one foot in front of another – and trying not to stand on any venomous snakes.

He paused for a moment, then lengthened his stride and moved on. The reptile he had almost stepped on observed him through eyes darker than any night but made no move to strike.

He by then was wondering if this damn jungle was ever going to end, and was taken by surprise when it suddenly did.

Harrow was out in the open. The sun blazed down on him and he had to shield his eyes.

He heard Fast Eddie say, "Wow!"

Harrow blinked, his vision adjusting to the sudden glare and, now he could see clearly, he felt the same way.

They had emerged to the sight of a gorge unravelling before them. A stream flowed along the center of the gorge, bordered by narrow rock-strewn strips of open ground. Beyond these there were patches of undergrowth, then sheer cliffs rising up on either side of the gorge, essentially trapping them within its confines.

Harrow smiled to himself. He did not feel trapped. He believed that if it was possible to head west along this gorge, they could reach the base of the precipice and the things that lay there. Gold coins scattered among the bleached bones of thieves.

He turned to JJ and nodded in the direction he wanted them to go. "I'd say our destination is three days that-a-way as the crow flies."

"So, another week minimum as the grunt stumbles." JJ looked shattered as he said this, though he wore a smile.

Things were looking up but they needed to rest.

"We'll make camp here until the morning," Harrow said.

Everyone appeared too tired to even acknowledge this, but backpacks were unstrapped and dropped and left to lay where they had fallen. Boots were unlaced and pulled off, along with socks that were more holes than fabric. Salgado Joe grimaced as he examined his blistered bare feet.

Sitting close by, Fast Eddie acted as if he was about to puke. From behind his hand he said, "You sure know how to spoil a beautiful moment, Salgado. Your feet stink!"

Salgado Joe held one of his boots up and

threatened to throw it at Fast Eddie.

But both men were grinning.

Harrow left them to it. He could feel the tension easing in his aching limbs and began to unpack his sleeping bag. The sun was close to the edge of the narrow horizon and he wasn't sure if he'd even make it to nightfall before he'd turn in.

He had the feeling he would sleep well for the first time in a long time as he sat down by the side of his sleeping bag and started to take his own boots off.

Before he went to sleep, though, he needed to eat. Fast Eddie was building a fire from small snapped off branches. Thick, gray smoke was spiraling off the wood because it was too damp to light properly. Fast Eddie stamped it out and went in search of better kindling.

The Banjo twins had also got themselves a branch. Harrow watched as they used their bayonets to slim and smooth it, whittle another piece of wood into a hook, and use vine to finish their improvised fishing rod off.

Harrow's mouth began to water. They'd been living off canned, processed, rubbery pork and sugary energy bars. It looked like fresh fish was on the menu for this evening's meal.

He settled back to wait.

Flies danced over the surface of the stream as one of the Banjo twins cast off. Harrow still couldn't tell them apart. He did not even know their names.

It was no big deal. Much more important was the fish they were hauling in. It was a good size, with a broad, flattened head and four large fins. Harrow had never caught one himself but he knew it was a lungfish.

He'd never eaten one either and, after the fish had been grilled slowly over the fire, he devoured his portion gratefully.

It was dark by the time the meal was finished and, with a full belly, Harrow crawled into his sleeping bag. He was looking forward to a good night's sleep, then seeing what the new day would bring.

CHAPTER 6

Harrow opened his eyes, yawned, rolled over, and saw claws inches from his face.

Suddenly wide awake, he sat bolt upright and wriggled backwards on his butt.

The claws belonged to a crab. It was a big, ugly son of a bitch, and it was crawling towards him, closing the distance his panicked shuffle had put between them.

Its pincers filled his vision. They were viciously serrated. One snap of those things could sever a man's finger, bone and all.

Harrow gulped, looked around for his knife, but it was out of reach. And next to his gun.

Damn! Hand to claw combat was not going to end well for him.

"Yo, Lieutenant!" Harrow looked up, just as one of the Banjo twins threw him a baseball bat.

He did not have time to think. He caught the baseball bat, grasped the handle tight and swung it with all his strength at the crab.

Which snapped its pincers shut over the bat, stopping it in its tracks.

Harrow grunted and tried shaking the crab free. But it wasn't letting go. So, he struggled to his feet and tried a new approach.

He lifted the baseball bat, and the clinging crab,

up to head height and began to swing them both around at speed.

It was enough to dislodge the crab, which went flying off through the air before coming tumbling back down to earth near the edge of the stream. It landed on its way too many legs and did not look hurt as it crawled down into the water.

Harrow slumped back down to the ground still holding the baseball bat as the Banjo twins wandered over.

"Interesting technique," one of them said.

Harrow laughed despite himself, then looked at the bat with a questioning expression on his face.

One of the twins responded, "You said you were looking for a baseball bat, so we made this when we couldn't sleep."

His brother added, "It's no big deal. We've always loved carving wood and there's plenty of raw material here."

Harrow rested the bat on his open palms. Its weight, its balance, felt perfect.

"This is fantastic craftsmanship," he told the twins. "You're wasted here. You should be running your own workshop."

The twins both cast their eyes downwards.

"Folk like us don't open workshops," one of them said.

The brother went on, "Folks like us drink and fight and end up dying young. Or joining the army or going to jail."

"Or both, in our sad-sack case."

"But you never know. With our share of the gold coins perhaps we can prove everyone wrong."

"Open our business and put our names above the door."

"What do you think, Lieutenant?"

"I think that sounds swell," Harrow replied and raised the baseball bat to his temple in a kind of salute.

They gave him a relaxed salute in return.

Old habits died hard.

Old prejudices harder still.

Wondering on this, Harrow started packing up his gear.

Salgado Joe and Fast Eddie had slept through his encounter with the crab and were only now stretching and sitting up. The Pastor seemed engrossed in counting out sticks of dynamite and muttering under his breath, and JJ was emerging from the undergrowth, nature's rest room.

"Coffee and chow and then we move out," Harrow said loud enough for them all to hear, then added, "And canned pork is fine." The idea of catching breakfast from the stream really did not appeal.

Thirty minutes later they were making good progress along the gorge. After days of struggling with a steep gradient, being on level ground felt so much easier.

Still, it was not a walk in the park.

"Keep focused on where you're putting your feet, people," Harrow said. "It would be real easy to twist an ankle or snap an ankle out here, and there's no ERs within crawling distance."

"No problem," Salgado Joe called ahead. "Fast Eddie's real slick on his feet, all the getaways he's done."

"You are one cheeky cur," Fast Eddie shot back. "I always drive away from the scene of a crime."

"I am going to be driven everywhere by a chauffeur when I'm rich," Salgado Joe went on with a distant look in his eyes. "A real beautiful chauffeur with long blond hair tucked up under her cap."

Harrow groaned. "I said, keep focused." Then he almost slipped because he wasn't following his own advice.

He'd been distracted by a dark shape flying low over the water.

Something was heading their way at speed.

Fast Eddie had seen it as well. He said in a halting voice, "It looks like a dragonfly, but... goddammit, it's big."

He was calling it like it was. What appeared to be a dragonfly was skimming the surface of the stream. But the span of its gossamer wings must have been close to two and a half feet. And as it came closer still, Harrow could see that its mandibles were lined with sharp teeth.

It was the strangest thing.

Harrow instinctively took a step back, even though the giant dragonfly was showing no signs it was aware of them.

In shocked silence, they all watched it fly on until it was a glint in the sunlight and then was lost to sight.

JJ was the first to find his voice.

"What the hell was that?"

"Some kind of supersized bug," Salgado Joe exclaimed.

"One ugly Mother!" Fast Eddie added.

The Pastor muttered darkly, "An abomination. That will burn in the cleansing flames."

"I prefer supersized bug," Salgado Joe said, deadpan.

Harrow's head was spinning. It wasn't just the insect's size that bothered him. It was those predator's teeth as well.

With no idea what else to do or say, he told them, "Let's keep moving."

They walked until the sun was directly overhead. Harrow was parched and, though he had no appetite, the others might need more sugary snacks or mega-processed pork.

"We'll take thirty," Harrow said. "Eat, crap, circle of life. Then we up the pace until dusk."

"You're a real sweetheart, Lieutenant," Fast Eddie said with a broad grin on his face then produced a can opener from his backpack.

While the others settled down to eat, the Pastor

sat to one side. He was muttering again, a quiet rant about the end of times.

Harrow kept a poker face as he listened.

The others were showing sides to themselves that Harrow liked. But the Pastor was starting to really disturb him. They were a small unit in alien territory. They had to trust each other.

Harrow moved over to JJ and whispered, "What's with the Pastor?"

JJ smiled sadly before answering. "He was an army chaplain. He worked at the heart of a host of combat zones. Wherever he was, whatever was happening around him, he was one of the genuine good guys. He always had time to sit down and listen, and provide comfort and advice. It did not matter if the soldier had faith or not. Then... I don't know for sure what happened, but I've always figured that he reached breaking point. Even the strongest can only take so much. He went from gentle and thoughtful to preaching about hellfire and damnation. And then just talking about it was not enough. He blew up an arms' dump. Sent a whole stack of munitions sky high and stood there with his arms outstretched while everyone else ran for cover. He was medically discharged after a spell in the slammer."

Harrow felt bad. It wasn't the first time he had heard a story such as this. About brave men broken by the horrors of war.

He puffed out his cheeks, and told JJ, "I'm truly

sorry to hear that."

JJ gave a slight shrug. "He's one of us now and if anything needs detonating, well, we don't need to wait for divine intervention. We've got our man on the ground."

Then JJ patted Harrow on the shoulder and added, "None of us are poster boys, Lieutenant."

"I hear you," Harrow replied wistfully, "And by the way, JJ..."

He paused.

On top of everything else, Harrow kept meaning to say that there was no need to call him Lieutenant. Trouble was, he had realized he liked it. He was missing having rank, a uniform, the structure the army provided.

For all the collateral damage, it had been his life.

"You okay there, Lieutenant?" JJ asked, breaking into Harrow's thoughts.

Harrow decided to leave the Lieutenant chat for another time, smiled, and said, "All good. Now lets round them up and move them on."

The break had not cooled any of them down.

As the day wore on, the temperature just rose and rose. Sweat pooled inside Harrow's boots and stuck his clothes to his skin. When this was over, he was going to burn everything he wore and spend hours in the shower, while drinking one cold beer after another.

He wiped a hand across the back of his lips and dragged himself on through the harsh landscape.

They had seen no signs that anyone else had been there. And people usually left traces. Once, early in his army days, Harrow had used his leave to go climbing with a couple of friends. They'd reached a peak with a stunning view of the land for miles around – only all Harrow could see was the crushed cola can and plastic wrapper that had been discarded on the ground.

Some people could be real jerks.

If Harrow and his comrades were the first to walk this gorge, that was swell by him. And they would not be leaving any of their crap behind. He would make sure of that.

Harrow winced, swatted something stinging the back of his neck, and wiped the bloody smear left behind onto his trouser leg but only made it worse.

Bloody bugs. There was no shortage of those. All regular sized though. There had been no more giant insects. Or crabs with vicious pincers.

Just bugs everywhere and the sound of rustling in the undergrowth nearby.

It was all fine.

"A moment of your time, Lieutenant."

It was Fast Eddie. He was crouched over, peering at something on the ground.

From where Harrow stood, he thought it was just a small rock. Another rock in the crowd. He strolled over anyway and saw he was completely wrong.

Fast Eddie was peering at a skull. Its bones tapered out to form a snout. Sharp teeth lined the jaws.

"The rest of it is here."

Salgado Joe was waving the others over to where he stood nearer the undergrowth.

The remainder of the skeleton lay there. Harrow's attention was drawn to vicious looking sickle-shaped claws extending from its hind feet. As for the rest of the remains, the tell-tale signs of tooth marks on some of the larger bones stood out to him.

Its flesh must have been stripped from its bones. By its killer first most likely. Scavengers would have followed. The insects would have finished the process.

Harrow rubbed the stubble on his chin, thinking hard.

He tried to reconstruct the animal in his mind, tip it back up onto its feet and set it running. He thought it could have stood perhaps shoulder height with an average man – gut level for Salgado Joe.

But he had never seen remains like these and had no idea what the creature had been.

It was another strange inhabitant of the gorge. Well, ex-inhabitant.

Instinctively, Harrow glanced around.

It was logical to assume there were other creatures like this alive nearby.

And whatever had predated it.

Harrow stepped away.

Salgado Joe stayed close, patting his belly as he spoke, "Dang. Must have been some good meat on that critter. Would have made for fine eating. Barbecued nice and slow over an open fire."

There was a lot of Salgado Joe so it was fair enough he thought about his belly first.

Harrow still had no appetite at all. He had a rifle slung over his shoulder, a knife in a holster at his belt and the baseball bat in his hand and ready to swing.

"Eyes wide open, boys," he said. "I'm not sure if the local wildlife will know Salgado Joe is top of the food chain. Now, let's get a few more miles in before we make camp for the night."

CHAPTER 7

Harrow woke in the night to the sound of thunder. He lay there listening as a distant noise rolled towards him through the darkness once more.

A chill ran over his skin.

It was not thunder.

It was a roar.

Harrow did not move. He lay there trying to take regular, calming breaths.

He had spent nights in deserts trying to sleep as missiles rained down on enemy positions nearby. On concrete floors in the shells of homes as the injured cried out for help, knowing he could not answer their calls because there were snipers with night-vision sights waiting for any sign of movement. In jungles, not so different to the one they had passed through to reach the gorge, listening for footsteps which meant someone was coming with death on their mind and a sharp blade gripped tight in their hand.

Lying there, listening as another primal roar filled the night, felt worse than any of those things.

In desert, city and jungle he had been gripped by fear. But he had understood the dangers waiting for him. Here, in this gorge, he was facing terrors unknown.

He listened, waiting for the next roar, but it did

not come. And, somehow, he must have fallen asleep again, because the next thing he knew it was sunlight breaking through into his dreams.

He blinked, shifted around, scratched his bitten face. He felt more tired than he had when he'd climbed into his sleeping bag, and more on edge.

Part of him just wanted to stay there, to curl up and go back to sleep and not have to face the new day. But in the end a full bladder forced him to drag himself out of his sleeping bag and go find a private spot to relieve himself.

He took the baseball bat with him.

When he got back, the others were stirring. Salgado Joe stumbled out of his sleeping bag, went over to the stream, stripped off, got in the water buck naked and started to wash himself.

Harrow would have preferred the sight of another crab at the start of a new day.

Thinking of which...

Harrow had not told Salgado Joe about the crab and its vicious pincers. One snap of those things and a man could be diminished for life.

Salgado Joe lay down in the stream to fully immerse himself, then stood back up and headed back to the rocks.

No damage done. The lady who'd thought Salgado Joe 'exotic' would have been relieved.

Starting to feel brighter, Harrow went to get fueled up for the day.

It was going to be another blisteringly hot one.

Harrow wondered if there was any other kind of day around here as he finished off his cup of coffee by sloshing the last of the bitter, dark liquid around like mouthwash.

He spat it out, and said, "Let's go find ourselves some gold."

There was a tired 'whoop' from Fast Eddie, smiles from the Banjo twins. The Pastor was silent. JJ raised a thumb. Salgado Joe scratched his balls then finished pulling his trousers up.

Harrow hitched his backpack on and set off.

A spider with two red dots on its back scurried out from a crack in a rock by his feet. Red for 'don't mess with me'. Harrow had no intention of doing that and moved slightly to one side so the spider could crawl on unimpeded.

Then someone swore. Someone said, "We've got company."

Thinking it might be another spider, maybe even a supersized one, Harrow turned to look.

He was relieved to see it was not a threatening arachnid.

The 'company' was the size of a small pig. It might have been a distant cousin of a pig. A cousin that had bred with other cousins over many generations. It was ugly as sin. Two short tusk-like teeth poked out of the side of its mouth and a clump of wiry gray hair stood up at the base of its head.

It was also trotting over towards Salgado Joe.

Harrow wondered if the big man was going to

suggest a barbecue, but even he didn't seem to think the pig thing was appetizing.

He was backing away from it instead, trying to shoo it off. But the pig thing was not taking the hint. It moved right up to Salgado Joe and nuzzled its snout against the side of his calf.

Leaving a smear of pig thing gunk.

"Jeez," Salgado Joe grumbled. "Will you get lost, pal!"

Fast Eddie was the first to laugh out loud.

"You've got a little friend," JJ said.

"More than a friend."

"I think its love."

This from the Bingo twins, who were grinning wickedly as well.

Even the Pastor might have had a slight smirk on his face.

"Yeah man," Fast Eddie threw in. "Hope we're all invited to the wedding."

"Quit it!" Salgado Joe yelled. Whether this was to the pig thing, which was taking a keen interest in his boot laces, or to his comrades, Harrow didn't know.

Salgado Joe did an ungainly pirouette to take his laces away from the pig thing's snout and teeth and started to walk away.

The pig thing followed him with its eyes. Harrow had to admit it did look like the creature had taken a shine to the big man.

"The runt will lose interest in you soon," JJ said.

"When it gets to know you," Fast Eddie added and guffawed at his own joke.

Salgado Joe kept his head down, kept walking, while the pig thing kept following.

Harrow smiled. It felt good. It had been a while.

He made his way back to the front of the company – and its four-legged plus one.

A couple of miles or so later the pig thing was still with them but it was falling behind. Likely due to its stumpy legs.

Salgado Joe was hesitating, looking back. To Harrow's amazement he went up to the pig thing, took out a water bottle and poured some of its contents into his cupped hand, then leaned over. He had to lean a long way.

The pig thing lapped at the water in his hand thirstily.

Salgado Joe raised himself back up to his full height, took a drink directly from the bottle himself, them looked around at the others. "What?" he asked.

The kind of 'what' that precedes many a fight in many a bar on a Friday and a Saturday night all over the world.

There were smiles, shrugs, but no more making fun of the big man for now.

Harrow thought how a break to take onboard more liquids, and some eats, was a good idea for all of them. His own mouth was bone dry and his guts were rumbling belatedly.

He looked around for a good spot – and saw a sudden flash of darkness in the sky. Wings cutting through the air. Claws extending.

And the pig thing was caught and being carried up off the ground by – Harrow could not say.

The bogey had a long, sharp beak and large, dark eyes. A bony crest spiked out from the back of its skull. Its slender, leathery wings – which had a span of six feet, maybe more – made him think of a bat, of a reptile, rather than a bird.

The pig thing in its grasp was screaming in fear and struggling to get free.

Salgado Joe was hollering as well. Not any words that Harrow could make out. Just shouting furiously, helplessly.

Fast Eddie had a rifle aimed. Hesitating to take the shot. Maybe wondering if he'd hit the pig thing.

Harrow thought it would not be so bad if he did. At least it would put the poor creature out of its misery.

Though that moment had gone. The pig thing was loose somehow, falling.

A gun shot rang out. Not Fast Eddie, Harrow saw when he spun around. It was Salgado Joe who had fired. He started to lower his gun.

Job done.

The bogey was spiraling to earth. It crashed onto rocks. One wing-tip hung out over the stream.

That wing was still moving, the other one seemed spent. The head flopped around on its long, thick neck.

It was in its death throes.

Salgado Joe clearly wanted to hurry it over the line. He was striding over – but no, Harrow was wrong again.

The big man was going to the pig thing, which lay on its side nearby not moving. He went down on one knee and placed a hand tenderly on its side.

No one said anything. A couple of them looked away. Fast Eddie swore. He was looking up into the sky.

Six more of the bogeys were descending at speed.

Guns were raised in response, aimed.

Harrow held up a hand, called out, "Hold fire."

He could see where the dirty half-dozen were heading.

And they did descend onto their stricken kin. They tore at it with their claws and teeth-lined beaks. They ripped, they butchered.

Harrow could see the bogey they were attacking was still alive. It raised its head and tried to lash out with its own beak. But it did not stand a chance.

Harrow turned away, not wanting to see any more. He noticed Salgado Joe was carefully, gently, placing rocks over the body of the pig thing.

When he'd completely covered it, he straightened up, wiped the sweat from his brow and said, "I know this is stupid. I know the bugs will be able to get at it, probably other scavengers will come along and dig it out, but I don't want those damn flying freaks to touch it."

Harrow glanced back at the six bogeys. They had finally finished their feast.

They were looking over towards Salgado Joe, curious, maybe wondering if they could make their move on the still warm corpse under the rocks.

Harrow wasn't humanizing these things. He could see it in their eyes.

He raised his own gun, fired a round of automatic close to where they stood.

They understood that well enough. They scattered, and flew higher, higher, until they were just shapes in the brilliant blue sky.

Fast Eddie was stood alongside Harrow, his neck craned. "You should have wasted them, Lieutenant," he said without looking down.

Harrow nodded.

Next time he would.

CHAPTER 8

Over the course of the stifling, sullen hours that followed the gorge started to widen. The rock faces still rose almost vertically on either side, and the stream flowed towards them, a lone artery, while the undergrowth spread closer. It grew denser and higher. It was becoming a jungle, with its vines twisting tight as garottes, its narrow trees clawing at the air.

To Harrow, despite the fact that the gorge was widening, it started to feel more claustrophobic – and threatening.

There was the constant rustle of movement in the rising jungle. Out of sight, but in mind. Scraping away at his nerves and fueling his imagination.

The encounters they'd had so far had been strange and disturbing. Only the brain dead would not have wondered what else might be out there.

From their strained expressions, the others were increasingly concerned as well.

Or maybe it was just the evil heat and the plague of bugs. Good old down to earth torments that were in their faces and clear as day.

Harrow paused to take a sip of water. It was hot and tasteless and did nothing to quench his thirst.

He splashed a few more drops onto the back of his neck. There was a microsecond of relief and then the sun continued to rotisserie him.

He shielded his eyes from the glare to check the position of the sun. Unless he had got this hideously wrong, the gorge should still be leading them to the base of the precipice.

He felt he was correct, nodded to himself. Then around the edge of his vision, he noticed dark shapes. Wings.

There were more flying reptiles. Bogeys. Were they the same ones from earlier? Were they following, waiting for the right moment to attack, and feed?

Or were they new?

Either way he did not like these soaring forms, casting their fleeting shadows on the world beneath.

But there was no way to shake them off. And mighty tempting as it still was, he decided that loosing a few rounds their way at that moment in time would have been an unacceptable waste of ammunition. They needed to conserve their supply.

Harrow made a gun from his hand instead, put pressure on an imaginary trigger.

"Take that, you son of a bitch," he said out loud.

JJ looked up. "Those things give me the creeps," he said.

"Me too," Harrow replied.

"The supersized dragonfly was weird enough, but those bastards. Jeez!" JJ shivered despite the heat of the day before adding, "What is it about this place and its screwed-up wildlife?"

Harrow was trying to think of an answer that made sense and getting nowhere fast, when Fast Eddie said, "I got myself a theory. It's out-there looney-tunes but so is what we've seen. I think this place is a closed eco-system."

"A what?" JJ asked.

Fast Eddie took a sip of water before answering, "The wildlife in this gorge has had little or no interactions with living beings from outside its borders for a long time. As a result, there has been no need for it to adapt over that time period, been no extinctions either."

"You mean they've all just stayed the same?" one of the Banjo twins asked.

"Just stayed in one placed and bred with each other," his brother added.

"Sounds like my home town," Salgado Joe said with a wry grin.

JJ did not look convinced. "Sounds pretty messed up to me," he said. "And besides, Fast Eddie, where did you hear about closed echo-systems?"

"Eco-systems," Fast Eddie replied. "This police cell I was in down mid-western way. The jail was a real small place. I could see the TV the deputy watched all day through the bars, and the fellow loved the nature and science channels. I guess I picked myself up a useful education while I was locked up."

"I guess," JJ said, still sounding unsure. "So,

you're saying that explains the strange critters we've been seeing. Including those flying freaks."

Fast Eddie didn't sound so sure himself when he answered, "That's where we cross over into madman territory. I'm thinking that this place has not seen real change for more than a few decades, or even centuries. I think it's as it was thousands of years ago, and as for those flying things... well, you boys ever heard of terrible lizards?"

There was an uncomfortable silence until Salgado Joe said, "You mean dinosaurs?"

Fast Eddie simply nodded. He was starting to squirm with embarrassment, looking like he was wishing he had kept his mouth shut.

"Sorry," he said. "It was just what I saw on TV."

"It is not a problem," Harrow told him, not wanting Fast Eddie to feel bad.

"The deputy was also partial to shows about UFOs," Fast Eddie went on, speaking quicker and quicker. "I know about them as well. How they kidnap folk and probe them where it..."

Harrow cut him off, saying in as calm a voice as he could, "It's fine. Let's focus on the job at hand, people. If there are more big, ugly critters out there, as long as they don't get in our way, I don't care why they're there and what they are. Now, less talk, more miles covered. This is a treasure hunt not a debating club. Move out!"

There was no backchat. Harrow set a faster pace. There was a rustle in the jungle to his right. A cry overhead. Harrow's fingers tightened around the baseball bat.

He studied the edge of the jungle, but could see nothing moving through it. He looked to his left, over the stream.

Nothing there.

No, wait.

There was a shape among the foliage. Something moving at speed on long hind legs.

Then it was gone.

Salgado Joe had seen it as well. He had his gun aimed.

"Conserve your ammunition until we are facing a direct threat," Harrow ordered.

Salgado Joe held his gun in place. "I'd rather shoot first and ask if it has a good sense of humor and likes old movies later."

Harrow did not raise his voice. His tone brokered no argument, though: "No, Salgado."

The big man looked disappointed but lowered his weapon. He was squinting into the distance. "Lost it anyway," he said.

Harrow had as well.

For all of two minutes.

"Critter at six 'o' clock."

Alerted by this call out from Fast Eddie, Harrow had the creature back in his sights. Through rare gaps in the tangled growth he could make out enough this time to believe it was a live specimen of the skeleton they'd found.

No doubt there were nature geeks who could have told you its name and what it ate. This terrible lizard. This dinosaur with deadly sickle-shaped claws on its hind legs.

Harrow didn't care what it was called but he had to wonder if its diet would include ex-soldiers marinated in sweat.

If it emerged from the jungle and started heading their way, he would order targeted fire once it reached the stream, because from the glimpses he was getting the creature looked like it could take a man down.

It did – as he had tried to picture from the skeleton – stand head height with him. And as for those claws...

Even the brief looks he was getting at them was sending shivers through his frame.

"Another critter at three 'o' clock."

Harrow looked that way, exhaled when he saw JJ had not been seeing ghosts.

This critter was out in the open. Close enough to see clearly. Its eyes were small and set below a bony ridge. Gray tough-looking scales covered its body. There were a few dark feathers clinging to its frame as well. Whether they were feathers that remained after the creature had shed, or that had been picked up from a recent kill, Harrow did not know.

Did not give any more thought to.

His gaze had been drawn back to its claws.

One stab of those would leave a man crippled,

bleeding out. One slash would eviscerate. Same result. You'd die slowly, in agony – if you'd been left.

But wild animals did not kill for fun. Only man did that.

If this creature struck with its claws it would feed on its victim. Alive or dead would make no difference.

"If either of those things attacks take them out," he said to no one in particular, then walked on.

The critters did not attack. They followed. An hour after they'd first been sighted, a third and then a fourth appeared.

They all kept their distance.

Fingers rested close to triggers ready to fire if that changed.

CHAPTER 9

Dusk saw the sky streaked with red and the critters had grown in number.

Harrow counted ten of them moving at the edges of the jungle.

"Must be starved of entertainment round here, if we're such a big draw," JJ said, forcing a smile.

"Or just plain starved." Salgado Joe did not smile as he spoke.

Harrow patted the butt of his rifle. "We've got this. Now let's make camp for the night."

No one looked happy about this.

"We'd rather keep moving, Lieutenant," the Banjo twins said in unison.

"Me too," Fast Eddie added his opinion.

Harrow put his foot down. "Traveling in the dark over unknown territory is too risky. We make camp. We control and defend our position. End of."

Fast Eddie seemed like he was about to argue. Harrow stared him down then looked the others in the eye one by one. There were no more protests.

"Good," Harrow said. "First thing, we need to build a fire. There's enough kindling to hand without going far. Next, we mark out a boundary using rocks. Everyone is to stay inside the boundary at all times. If anyone needs to relieve themselves point it towards the boundary or squat and bury it afterwards. We will post sentries. We will all do shifts. When you are off duty, try and sleep. Let's get to it, people."

He asked the Banjo twins to take the first sentry shift, Fast Eddie to stack rocks at intervals in a rough circle around the camp, JJ to gather wood and start the fire and Salgado Joe to sort out the food. He left the Pastor rummaging intently through a backpack. Harrow really needed to unload.

By the time he had finished and buried the evidence, it was almost dark. Clouds obscured most of the sky but the fire JJ was building up was throwing out some light.

Maybe fire alone would be enough to keep the critters in their place.

Hoping this, Harrow finished buckling his belt and looked around to see how everyone else was doing.

He felt a flash of anger and asked, "Where is the Pastor?"

There was no sign of him.

"Moseying over now," JJ answered, and Harrow saw the Pastor was striding through the darkness towards them.

When he crossed the boundary, Harrow stepped into his path. "I made it very clear that everyone was to stay within the camp."

The Pastor clasped his hands together. "I answer to a higher power."

Harrow wanted to give a measured response,

save hollering for when he really needed to, so started counting up to ten by tapping the baseball bat against the side of his boot. He had reached eight when JJ put a hand on his shoulder and said quiet enough that only the two of them could hear, "A little leeway, Lieutenant. Please."

Harrow rested the end of the baseball bat on the top of his boot.

The moment had gone anyway.

He glared at the Pastor then went to check in with the Banjo twins. They had split up and were walking circuits around the boundary. At intervals, they clicked on flashlights and played the beams across the rocks, the jungle beyond.

He approached the nearer of the two.

"You okay there, Lieutenant?" the twin asked.

"I am. Only, I still can't tell you two apart. Figure it would be helpful if I could."

The twin grinned. "I'm Dwayne, my brother is Grant. Apart from our names, we're pretty much the same as far as other folk can tell."

Harrow held out a hand to shake. "Tom. Glad to have you along for the ride, Dwayne. Same goes for your brother."

They shook, then Harrow asked, "Anything to report?"

"Seems quiet out there. Let's hope it stays that way."

"Absolutely. You'll be relieved in a couple of hours."

Dwayne gave him a casual salute then carried on his way. His brother paused and they caught up, chatted for a minute, then went their separate ways again. Dwayne was on Harrow's right, Grant on his left.

Or was it the other way around?

Harrow had already got them mixed up and had no idea which was which. Laughing at himself, Harrow went to grab a couple of hours shut eye.

He took his boots off, unrolled his sleeping bag and crawled inside. He could feel the warming glow of the fire on his face, could hear the wood spitting out fiery fragments. Saw them drifting like fireflies in the darkness.

He rolled over, closed his eyes and began to drift himself.

The sound of an explosion pulled him back from the brink of sleep.

He sat up, spluttered, "What the hell?"

Fast Eddie and Salgado Joe were getting to their feet, looking groggy and shocked in equal measure. JJ was sprinting towards the Banjo twins. The Pastor had his hands clasped and his head bowed in prayer.

Harrow hurried after JJ. He was standing between the twins, who were directing their flashlights out over the rocks.

They illuminated blood and gore spread across the ground. There were chunks of flesh that could have been from anything. Then Harrow saw a sickle-shaped claw. It was whole but emerging from a length of hind leg that ended in a ragged, bloodied mess.

He was looking at the remains of one of the clawed dinosaur critters – after it had got up close and personal with high explosives.

Harrow turned, stared at the Pastor.

He'd stopped his praying. Had that dark smile on his face Harrow had seen before. He hadn't liked it the first time he saw it. He liked it even less now.

"What did you do?" he asked.

The Pastor spread his hands wide. "I placed pressure activated buried explosive devices around the camp. Praise be. No evil shall walk this way without facing the wrath of TNT."

Harrow did not tap out ten to try and hold his temper in check. "You should not have laid traps," he growled. "Not without my say-so."

The Pastor showed no signs he was going to say anything in his defense.

It was JJ who did this. "I'm not disagreeing with you, Lieutenant. But you have to admit the Pastor blitzed that dino critter, claws and all, to kingdom come. And if its buddies have any sense in their skulls, they will keep their distance now."

Maybe they would. Maybe they wouldn't. Harrow was still too wound up to want to debate the issue.

And suddenly distracted by a cacophony of screeching.

In the beams of the multiple flashlights that were suddenly being shone, he could see bogeys were descending on the slaughterhouse the rocks had become. He couldn't tally up how many there were because of the way they were now going after what was left of the critter.

They were in a feeding frenzy, frantically grabbing at chunks of flesh, and fighting with each other to get the biggest mortals. Two of the bogeys were having a tug of war over a length of flesh. Others were trying to take off with a blood-soaked morsel in their beaks, only to be attacked by more bogeys and made to drop their catch.

It was utter carnage.

And it could get worse.

Harrow took a couple of deep breaths, asked the Pastor in measured tones, "How many traps did you lay?"

"A dozen. And blessed each one."

"And at first light will you remember where you put them so none of us accidentally step on one and go meet our maker?"

"Of course," the Pastor replied without missing a beat. "I am not an amateur."

Harrow pretended he did not see the smiles on the others' faces. "First light," he said and walked away with every ounce of dignity he could muster.

He thought there was no way he was going to get any sleep.

He managed to doze, until the sound of a second

explosion a while later. Lying there, wide awake once more, he was still annoyed at the Pastor for not following orders, but had to admit that blowing the bastards up was an effective way to keep the men safe.

Whatever gets you through the night.

Thinking this, he finally fell fast asleep.

CHAPTER 10

Harrow's spell on sentry duty was relatively uneventful. Nothing else was blown to bits. But Salgado Joe talked in his sleep. Started saying after a while, "Oh, yeah, baby do it like that."

Fast Eddie who was on guard alongside Harrow muttered, "Permission to gag him, Lieutenant."

"Tempting," Harrow replied.

Thankfully for all concerned, Salgado Joe said nothing more as dawn arrived gray and still.

Harrow expected the mist would burn off and the cruel, unfiltered heat would return. Until then, he enjoyed the relative cool and looked around as the others woke up.

In the hazy morning light, he could see flies massed over two large swathes of the rocks. The insects hid the blood beneath left when the two clawed critters had been blown up.

There was no sign of anything else out on open land, nothing skulking in the undergrowth either that he could see.

The other critters it seemed had taken the high explosive hint and cleared out.

The bogeys still circled high above.

Harrow didn't care about them so much. His priority was making tracks.

He turned to the Pastor, said, "Hey, time to clear

your traps."

The Pastor acknowledged him with a wave of the hand then left the camp and went straight to a rock that looked like all the others to Harrow. When the Pastor started to lift out wire and a bundle of dynamite, it became clear the traps had been well hidden.

Harrow counted as seven more traps were made safe by the Pastor – leaving the way clear for them to move on.

Harrow held a thumb up to acknowledge the Pastor as he trudged back towards the camp.

The Pastor nodded.

Harrow wanted coffee. Five minutes to drink that, max. Pack his bag.

The Pastor stopped, knelt to tie a bootlace.

Harrow swore. Raised his rifle. Fired once.

He hit the critter, which had burst out of the undergrowth and was racing towards the Pastor, in its throat.

Its head flailed.

The Pastor flinched.

Harrow fired again. It was a superb shot. A total fluke, but he was not complaining as the critter fell onto its side and lay there twitching for a few moments.

A last spasm and it was still.

Fast Eddie howled in triumph and started to run towards it.

"Get back," Harrow yelled. "Pastor, on your feet

and over here as well."

He looked up, expecting to see the bogeys spiraling down to feed on this fresh kill.

But the sky was empty.

He did not understand why.

"Where have they gone?" JJ asked. He was peering up into the sky as well.

Harrow shook his head. Scratched his stubble. Wondering.

Then Salgado Joe said, "Incoming."

And Harrow understood.

The others had made themselves scarce because there was a new bogey in town. Just one. It did not need strength in numbers.

It was massive, must have measured twenty feet across its wings.

It had the same short neck and long beak as the others, and could be it was related. He might ask Fast Eddie later, see if there'd been an episode on the jail's TV about this thing.

Later.

Most important thing there and then was backing slowly away. Hissing orders at the others to do the same.

The bogey was not paying any attention to them. But he did not want to risk catching its eye with sudden movements.

He wanted it to keep on its current course – down towards the corpse.

It did, and with a surprisingly graceful sweep of

its vast wings landed on the rocks next to the critter Harrow had taken out. And then it began to feed. It tore open the dead body with its own sharp claws then ripped out glistening innards with its long, curved beak.

Harrow and the others crept away.

Ahead of them, the gorge grew wider still. Dense jungle rose higher up each side of the sheer rock-faces.

Meaning more cover. More eyes on them.

Was that paranoia? Harrow did not think so.

And to make matters worse, the regular bogeys were back. High overhead. Their six-foot long wings barely moved. They were riding the thermals. Waiting to strike.

It felt to Harrow like they were increasingly under siege.

Harrow scowled, tried to focus on the ground in front of his feet. Keep putting one foot in front of the other, find the gold, get the hell out of there.

He told himself this over and over as they approached a line of large brown mounds. They split in two to skirt the edges of the first one they reached.

Through a layer of encircling flies he could see fat, black bugs crawling through the pile of dung – there was no mistaking now that was what the mound was. It was not just the sights, it was the smell. Jeez! Harrow started to gag.

There were dozens of small bones in there as

well. Whatever kind of creature had crapped this out was bastard big and a meat eater.

Harrow was not the only one thinking this.

"If we meet this monster, keep out of range of its rear," Fast Eddie said.

They'd reached the next pile and gave that plenty of space as well as they walked past it.

"Imagine one of those landing on your head! Imagine dying like that!" Salgado Joe added.

Harrow could. Wished he hadn't and walked on.

Without warning, there was a loud rustling sound to his right. The crack of branches breaking.

Seven safety catches were released.

A head appeared through the jungle.

Harrow's mouth opened but no words came out. He'd been expecting a new terror to be unleashed. Not this.

The face that had been revealed was strangely simple. Small eyes sat over a short, flat snout. The creature's neck was as wide as the head, and incredibly long. Fifteen feet give or take. Its torso and wide legs looked made for lumbering slowly along, which was what they were doing.

As for its tail – Harrow had thought the neck was long, but the tail did not look like it was ever going to end.

When all of the creature was finally out of the undergrowth and stomping slowly over the rocks, it was the length of a basketball pitch.

"Remember, if it points its ass at you, run like

hell," Salgado Joe said.

Fast Eddie grinned. "Still good advice, but those droppings are not from this dinosaur. This one is a plant eater so there'd be no animal bones in its crap. I saw a CGI recreation of it on one of the TV shows I watched in the jail. They said about its diet and that it was one of the dumbest dinosaurs to ever walk the earth. Got a tiny brain inside that slip of a skull and that the reason it survives is because it's too dang big to hunt down and eat."

Harrow could believe that. It was looming over them as it came closer.

"So, what you're saying is that were safe"? JJ asked.

"Long as you step sharpish to one side so as not to get stood on, yep, you're good."

They all cleared a path, a substantial path, for the giant dinosaur.

It did not appear to have even noticed them as it made its way to the stream, where it began to drink.

"It got a name?" asked one of the Banjo twins – possibly Dwayne, or was it Grant? Honestly, Harrow still had no idea.

"It's a kind of sauropod, I think," Fast Eddie answered after a long pause to think. "Yes, I'm sure that's it."

"Sounds like a crock of the stuff lying over there," Salgado Joe said.

"No, really, I seen it on TV."

"How long did you spend in that particular jail?"

Harrow asked. "Seems like you did some serious viewing time."

A crooked smile spread across Fast Eddie's face. "I was what you might call a repeat guest, Lieutenant. You see, at the time I had some real bad dudes on my back. For some reason they seemed to think I'd ripped them off and they were after breaking all my bones and leaving me in a ditch. Well, whenever the heat got too bad, I'd get myself arrested by the same deputy and lie low for a while in his jail. It was safe and I got my four squares a day."

"And did they ever say on the shows about dinosaurs still being alive and kicking?"

"No, Lieutenant. They were all wiped out a long time ago."

Harrow looked up at the giant dinosaur still slurping away at the stream. "Apart from here," he said, lost in thought.

For the first time since they had entered the gorge, he felt a sense of wonder. This giant was the most incredible thing he had ever seen. And the fact that it existed, the fact he was able to witness it first hand was surely a privilege.

As he stood watching with a dopey grin on his face, the sauropod raised its head from the stream and began to swing its stunning bulk around.

Shadows covered the ground beneath it as it made its way slowly back to the undergrowth, utterly oblivious of the seven figures looking up at it with their mouths hanging open.

"Epic," JJ said quietly.

CHAPTER 11

It was late afternoon, and he was back in a bleak frame of mind.

Dark clouds had drifted over the sun and the humidity was off the scale. It felt like they were in a pressure cooker. It was cruel punishment, close to unbearable.

Harrow would have wept but he was all dried out.

Even prison had been better than this. Having a staring contest with a cockroach that had crawled out of his cell's toilet bowl had been better than this.

One foot in front of the other.

He told himself this one more time, kept going. They passed a couple of the supersized dragonflies perched on rocks by the stream. Harrow saw blood on the teeth of one.

He licked his cracked lips, felt a stab of jealousy.

He had come close to losing his mind in prison.

Longing for blood to quench his thirst, and with the gorge stretching out in front of him and so frazzled he couldn't even think how far they had to go before they reached the base of the precipice, Harrow started to wonder if he was going to finally reach his breaking point out here.

One foot in front of the other... until he went insane.

He looked down at his boots to help will them on, saw a dark patch on the ground. Saw another one appear.

He had no idea what they were, but they were appearing faster and faster.

Harrow looked up and felt something strike his cheek. He raised his hand, touched his skin. It was wet.

He closed his eyes, tilted back his head and smiled as the rain ran down his face.

Close by he heard a whoop. Someone said, "Hallelujah."

Harrow opened his eyes and squinted through the rain to see JJ and Fast Eddie had joined hands and were dancing a jig.

Grinning from ear to ear, Harrow carried on with a spring in his step.

The rain fell in a deluge for hour after hour. It had worn out its welcome but they were making good progress so Harrow tried to ignore it.

"It can't go on for much longer," JJ yelled over the sound of the rain.

"Yep," Harrow shouted back, though he had his doubts. The rain, if anything, was getting heavier.

Harrow kept going until the downpour was so bad he couldn't even see the others.

It was no use. To go on would be too dangerous.

"Everyone stop where you are," he bellowed. "We will wait it out here." Then he stood there feeling like a drowned rat while the rain did its worst.

He wondered idly if any of the smaller dinosaurs were sheltering under the sauropod, smiled at the mental image this conjured up, and then, finally, thankfully, the rain started to ease off.

A few minutes later it stopped.

Harrow caught his breath, dripped. Looked up. And swore with joy.

In the distance he could see a dark shape rising above the clouds. It was the top of the precipice. The base, miles below, was shrouded in mist.

"Do you see that, Lieutenant!"

"I sure do," he replied, though he didn't know who to. He turned to look at the others. They were all soaked to the skin and beaming.

"The home straight," Fast Eddie said.

It was another couple of days of hard trekking before they reached their destination, Harrow figured. That felt like nothing now. They were on the right track. They were going to succeed.

He would have happily kept walking, but Salgado Joe and both of the Banjo twins were pulling off their boots and holding them upside down. Water flooded out.

JJ took of his t-shirt and started to wring it out.

Harrow glanced up at the sky. There wasn't a cloud in sight and he could already feel the sun growing warmer on the back of his neck.

"We'll take a break to get dry," he said and began to strip off himself.

The bugs had left no part of him that he could see untouched and his naked body was not a pleasant sight. The others were just as bad.

Luckily, the civilized world was a long way away, and there was no one who could be offended by the sight of them laying out all their clothes on the rocks to dry out.

He could see and hear movement in the jungle nearby and wondered what any dinosaurs looking out made of their first sight of humanity.

As nothing was trying to attack them, he figured, 'not very appetizing', was the answer.

Half a mile or so ahead, another of the sauropods briefly raised its head above the canopy. Further out, he could see bogeys taking to the air. They were the twenty-footers and their huge wings lifted them easily into the sky.

At this distance they were mighty impressive. Closer up, he would have been less keen.

He scratched the base of his spine. The bites went past there, inside, to where the sun did not shine.

"Bastard bugs," he muttered.

"Er, Lieutenant..." JJ said.

"What?"

"The scrawniest damn thing I ever did see is eyeing us up."

Harrow looked over to where Fast Eddie was pointing.

A creature of a type he'd never seen before had

emerged from the jungle.

In some ways, the newcomer resembled the clawed dinosaur critters which had stalked them the day before – it had the evil looking sickle-shaped claws protruding from its hind legs and a narrow snout with the tips of dangerously sharp teeth showing at the edges of its mouth.

But this thing was only as tall as a turkey and covered in feathers.

Well, mainly covered. Parts of it looked like it had been plucked. One of its eyes was missing as well.

It must have been in a few fights, this thing.

And its attention was definitely on them.

Harrow wasn't happy about that. He picked up the baseball bat and said, "Scram, pal."

The ragged beast, the scrawny 'saur, did the opposite.

It began to run towards them.

It was fast, was within biting distance of their legs before any of them could react.

But it wasn't after any of their limbs. It grabbed a pair of boxer shorts that had been drying in the sun in its mouth, then turned tail and sprinted back into the undergrowth.

"What the hell," Salgado Joe yelled furiously. "My shorts!"

He ran after the scrawny 'saur and disappeared into the jungle.

Moments later he backed out. His hands were

raised in front of his chest, his palms outstretched. He was moving very slowly, and staring intently into the foliage.

Where the one-eyed scrawny 'saur reappeared.

It didn't have Salgado Joe's boxer shorts in its mouth anymore.

He clearly didn't care about that. He was too busy staring at the dozens of scrawny 'saurs that were emerging from the undergrowth.

There must have been fifty of the turkey-sized terrors. A pack, bristling with claws and bared teeth.

They stood in a line and stared back.

Not attacking.

Yet.

Harrow would not have been worried if he and the others had been carrying their guns. But the guns were propped up by the clothes. They were a ten second dash away, another few seconds to pick up, aim, fire.

Time they might not have.

But they had to try.

He took a step back; as he did he saw a stick of dynamite spinning through the air towards the pack. It landed in their midst. Its fuse was burning down. The one-eyed scrawny 'saur stepped forwards and picked it up in its mouth.

It should have stuck to boxer shorts.

The explosion sent gore flying out in every direction. In its wake, feathers floated down.

Harrow glared at the Pastor. They'd been far too

close for comfort, could have been blown limb from limb as well.

But they had not been.

Once more, he had to admit the Pastor had saved their skin.

He took a deep breath, managed to gasp, "Thank you, Pastor."

Then he looked around to make sure no one was injured.

They were all splattered with gore, to which feathers had stuck. Apart from that they were still as naked as the day they were born.

CHAPTER 12

"Listen up. There's an hour of daylight left but I'd like us to start looking for a place to camp now. Somewhere we can fortify and defend for the night ahead. We all good with that?"

The bedraggled, bitten group nodded back at Harrow.

He moved over to JJ's side as they walked on and said in a quieter voice, "I am going to ask the Pastor to lay explosives in a ring around the camp. I'd like you to stay close to him as he does."

JJ raised an eyebrow and asked, "You don't fully trust him yet, despite him saving our asses a couple of times?"

"To be brutally honest, no."

JJ exhaled deeply. "You should. I do, absolutely. I thought I'd made that clear enough."

Harow looked over at the Pastor. He was keeping his distance from the others and talking to himself.

"Look," he said, turning back to JJ, "You heard about the man's history, his reputation. You were picking up intel. That's what you do. I get that."

JJ shook his head. "I did not learn about the Pastor second hand while we were both in prison. I met him before the horrors of war broke him."

He rubbed a hand across his eyes and took a deep breath before he continued. "I never served on the front line. I worked supplies, worked my schemes, but I was married to a solider who did. Her name was Mary-Anne and she was a medic. She could have stayed at a safe distance from the fighting if she'd chosen, and I begged her to do just that. But she wasn't having it. She was following her own path in life."

He hesitated, his voice beginning to break.

"That's one of the reasons I loved her. One of the many reasons."

He met Harrow's eye, smiled sadly. "So, yeah, she was out there at the sharp end, and one day she was preparing an injured soldier to be airlifted when there was a drone attack. She was badly injured. The type of bad you don't come back from. She did not die alone, though. The army chaplain sat with her and held her hand and talked to her. He told me this when he came to see me at the supply depot a week after she had passed. This was how I met the Pastor. He gave me her dog tag and a pendant she used to keep in her pocket and wear when she was off duty. She had asked to be buried with her wedding ring on, so, yeah, that was still with her..."

The hurt finally got too much and he could not go on.

"I am sorry," Harrow said.

He could not think what else to say.

Was still trying to think of something when Fast Eddie called out, "Hey Lieutenant, check this out. Higher ground, perfect to defend."

Harrow looked over to see Fast Eddie already scrambling up the steep, uneven sides of a large rocky mound.

From where he stood Harrow could not see the top, but it did look promising.

He hurried after Fast Eddie – who was finding it hard going – and Harrow soon caught up. They reached the top together.

Fast Eddie said, "Crap."

Harrow said nothing. He was transfixed by the coil after coil after coil of the snake curled up on top of the rocky mound.

It was immense. It could have swallowed a man down whole. Might not even have to dislocate its jaws to do this.

Fast Eddie said shakily, "Lieutenant, I think this spot is taken."

Harrow finally found his voice. "Yep."

As if it had heard them, the snake's head lifted and twisted towards them. Its tongue flickered out of its mouth. Its dark eyes glistened in the last of the sun's rays.

"I think we should leave."

"Yep."

They took a step back.

The snake began to uncoil.

They started to clamber back down the slope, not able to take their eyes off the nightmare vision rising before them.

When they reached the ground, the others were

rooted to the spot.

Apart from Salgado Joe. He raised his rifle, aimed it at the snake's head.

"You're only going to make it angry," one of the Banjo twins said.

"Even more angry," his brother added.

Salgado Joe lowered his rifle and said, "Yeah, you're right. Perhaps if we do nothing, it will curl back up. Now it's shown us who's boss."

He was wrong. The snake's head dipped and it began to slither down the slope, heading straight for them.

Harrow said in a calm voice, "Run."

He was not calm. He was actually very close to soiling himself as he turned tail and ran like hell.

The snake continued to unravel. It must have been thirty foot long. Harrow could not have sworn to that. Its tail was still on top of the mound as the rest of it moved across the ground.

Giving chase.

Or was it?

It seemed to be lingering, its head slightly raised, its devil's tongue reaching out.

Maybe it was trying to work out if they were worth pursuing?

Maybe it would decide they were not?

And this would turn out to be their lucky day.

No way he was going to stop and see, no way any of them were. They kept running – heading straight for the jungle.

If there had not been a monstrous snake pondering their fate, that would have been the last place Harrow would have run into.

A beggar not a chooser, he crashed through branches and vines, the fading sunlight cutting in and out as the canopy obscured the sky.

He could hear the others around him, could see them out of the corners of his eyes. They were not the first to pass this way. Felled trees lay all around, some snapped clean in half, some looked crushed underfoot.

He chanced a look over his shoulder, couldn't see the snake. He listened for it. All he could hear was the others gasping for breath.

But he still did not dare stop. He ran on. His lungs were bursting, his heart racing. His foot snagged in a root twisting out across his path. He stumbled, almost fell.

Salgado Joe caught him, hauled him upright.

JJ barreled past.

He was a dozen paces in front of them.

There one moment.

Gone the next.

Salgado Joe and Harrow sprinted forwards in time to see JJ falling into a deep, dark pit in the dirt.

He came to a halt next to the face of a dinosaur.

It was lying on its side. Nose to tail Harrow made it twenty-five feet long. Gray scales rippled out over its vast frame and a thick ridge rose like armor plating above the eye he could see.

The dinosaur looked lean and mean. A killing machine.

And asleep from the way its torso gently rose and fell.

But when it woke...

Not knowing how it hadn't when JJ had fallen in, not wanting to push their luck until it surely broke, Harrow whispered, "JJ."

JJ did not react. He was staring in horror at the dinosaur. He was breathing rapidly, clearly fighting not to lose it.

Screaming would be a bad idea. The last thing he ever did.

But no one could have blamed him if he had freaked out. That close he must have been able to feel the dinosaur's breath on his skin.

"JJ," Harrow tried again.

This time JJ shot him a glance.

'Climb out,' Harrow mouthed and waved his hands towards himself.

JJ looked back at the dinosaur. Its huge eyelid flickered, began to open.

Slowly slipped back closed.

Harrow started breathing again. He gesticulated frantically, a desperate mime.

And JJ must have got it now, because he started to clamber back up the side of the pit.

He was so slow. Needed to hurry.

The dinosaur's head twitched. A growl drifted from its mouth.

JJ seriously had to get a shift on.

Harrow fought to keep the mounting panic off his face as JJ crawled closer.

Harrow tried to give him an encouraging smile instead. A nod, a thumbs up.

And inch by painful inch JJ was getting there.

He had almost made it. Was almost safe.

Harrow stretched out an arm. JJ reached.

Then... there! Harrow had JJ's fingers in his, and was pulling him up. A final scrabble and he'd be out.

Harrow had not noticed the rock embedded in the lip of the pit – not until JJ's boot dislodged it and sent it tumbling down.

As they watched in horrified silence it seemed to fall in slow motion... then it bounced against the slope once and landed on the dinosaur's snout.

The dinosaur's eye shot open.

It stared straight at them.

They were in a world of trouble now. You didn't need to know a damn thing about dinosaurs to figure that out.

It was rising off the ground, using its tail as leverage, until it stood upright on its powerful hind legs.

It tilted its head down to once more fix them with its gaze, then it opened its mouth and roared.

It was the sound Harrow had mistaken for thunder. The sound of savagery unleashed.

It roared again. A gale of fetid air laced with

spittle struck them.

They all staggered backwards. Apart from JJ who was bent double projectile vomiting.

They couldn't wait for him to finish.

Harrow grabbed JJ by the collar and began to drag him away.

Leaving a trail of puke in their wake, they hot footed it out of there.

The dinosaur gave chase, its mass slamming down made the earth shake beneath their feet.

Harrow kept dragging JJ. All the strength seemed to have gone out of JJ's legs and bile was still dribbling from his lips. He was dead weight, slowing Harrow down, but he wasn't going to let go.

You did not leave anyone behind.

Salgado Joe had been ahead. He slowed. Leaned down, picked JJ up and put him over his shoulders in a fireman's lift.

Leaving Harrow free to run as a storm of primal fury closed in.

A few steps more and they burst back out into the open.

Within striking range of the snake.

It was still there, observing them through its dark, hooded eyes. Its tongue flickering. Its jaws opening, exposing vast fangs.

Fear rushed ice cold through Harrow's veins.

Ahead of him, the snake was poised.

Behind him, the T-Rex roared.

He had to act.

He spun to his right and began to run that way. The others followed his lead. He had no idea which way they were heading, just as long as it was away.

He glanced over his shoulder, to see the dinosaur emerge.

It saw the snake. Stopped dead in its tracks. Stared at the snake.

Harrow, Fast Eddie, the Pastor, the Banjo twins, Salgado Joe with JJ still draped over his shoulders stopped running. They had to see this.

Harrow felt like an insignificant speck as he stood there watching, as the snake swayed and hissed.

As the dinosaur crouched.

Attacked.

The dinosaur launched itself at the snake. It clamped its jaws around the snake's neck.

The snake tried to bury its fangs in the dinosaur, but could not get the angle for a clean strike.

One of its fangs struck the armored ridge above the dinosaur's eye without doing any harm that Harrow could see.

The dinosaur, its grip unrelenting, began to shake the snake's neck from side to side. The dinosaur's tail slid in arcs across the ground as it fought to keep its balance.

The snake was trapped, but not helpless. Its tail looped around the dinosaur's legs, its body wrapped around the torso, and it began to constrict. Within moments it had the dinosaur held in a vice-like grip.

The dinosaur's bones would be crushed, its bones broken, the life squeezed from it.

But it was not releasing its own hold on the snake's neck. It shook, it bit deeper, and blood began to trickle down the snake's scales.

The snake's head lifted. It seemed to be looking up into the sky. Its devil's tongue was hanging limply from its mouth.

The head fell back.

Toppled down to the ground.

The dinosaur had bitten clean through the snake's neck.

At a cost.

Its own head began to sway and Harrow believed it would have fallen if it had not still been held inside the corpse's coils.

Then the dinosaur seemed to recover. It lowered its jaws and began to gnaw through the highest coil. It fed as it freed itself, swallowing down fat chunks of snake meat.

No one had said a word during this spectacle.

Fast Eddie punctured the silence. He raised a fist to the heavens and cried out, "T-Rex, king of the dinosaurs. You rock!"

He arrowed a finger at the dinosaur.

The others grinned nervously, not sharing Fast Eddie's enthusiasm for the victor.

JJ tapped Salgado Joe on the shoulder and asked weakly to be let down.

Salgado Joe obliged and placed JJ gently onto his feet, keeping a hand on JJ's back just in case his legs gave way.

JJ seemed fine, though. Not recovered from his ordeal but on the way.

He looked over at the dinosaur as it freed its hind legs from the snake's remains and said, "Can we get out of here before that thing chews us up next."

"Chill, dude," Fast Eddie said brightly. "It's eating its fill and once it's done I think it will need to go lie down. We're safe."

"From it," JJ replied and spat out a last few drops of bile.

CHAPTER 13

They made camp without straying far. Looking for somewhere safe was too dangerous. The night was punctuated by explosions set off and gunshots taken – how many things they killed, how many winged, how many scared off they'd never know. Or even what they'd been shooting at in most cases.

Harrow had not slept a wink and felt dire. He scratched his scalp where bites had been bitten into by the unrelenting bugs and noticed a hair that had stuck to his finger and come loose was gray.

So much for his youthful good looks.

He wasn't going to be a captain by the time he was thirty, he'd be lucky if he wasn't totally decrepit the way his life was going.

Salgado Joe – whose looks must have had nothing to do with his supposed exotic charms – ran a hand across a skull that didn't even have a bristle and yawned.

"Time for eats," he said and looked out at the jungle on their side of the stream. "Don't suppose the scavengers will have left us any of our kills," he sighed.

Harrow stifled a laugh and told Salgado Joe, "We'll risk a trip into the jungle if you want, big man, be fine as long as we go mob handed and watch where we're stepping. I'm sure we can rustle up some berries or some roots for breakfast."

"Berries or roots!" Salgado Joe repeated. He looked utterly disgusted. Sounded it when he said, "We better get to that gold soon, Lieutenant."

Then he dragged himself wearily to his feet.

"Going to buy myself a burger joint and move in," he muttered as he moved off. "Buy a steakhouse and a place that does chicken wings in hot sauce and a pizza..."

Harrow shook his head and hauled his backpack on, as Salgado Joe trudged away still listing his edible dreams.

With the precipice in sight ahead to guide them, Harrow no longer took the lead. They were spread out, all on alert for any new threat.

Harrow still carried his baseball bat, every now and then taking a swing at an oversized bug that flew too close. The ones he managed to hit seemed to simply shrug the blow off and have another tilt at biting him.

The bogeys, like the bugs, remained a constant by day. The rustling of movement in the jungle did not let up.

They had not gone far however before Harrow forgot about all of them.

He could see the remains of a building in the distance. Meaning, the theory that they were the first people to come here was wrong.

But as they came closer, Harrow saw confirmation that humanity was, as first thought, only a sideshow here.

They were a blip. Passing through.

The large white slabs of the tail-bone stretched out over the rocks. They were bleached white by the sun. Beyond them, the ribs rose in sweeping arcs that reached fifty feet into the air.

Bewitched by them, Harrow stepped through a gap between two of the ribs and moved inside the gargantuan skeleton's torso. He felt like he had entered a derelict, ancient cathedral. The ribs could have been the last remnants of ceiling vaults.

The others had drifted in alongside him. Awe illuminated their faces, and the shadows cast by the ribs formed a lattice over the ground around them.

They walked on in silence until the neck vertebrae high overhead joined with the base of the skull.

There were bones in front of them that were cracked, collapsed. They scrambled over them and found themselves in the skull. It was cooler in this cavernous space. Light streamed in through the eye sockets and the gaps between the teeth, each of which was taller than Harrow.

There were dark corners, though.

The sound of movement.

Harrow clicked his flashlight on and directed the beam. It revealed a horned monster.

Two dark nubs protruded from the top of the dinosaur's head. Standing upright on its hind legs it was eye to eye with Harrow.

And it was snarling. Showing lines of jagged teeth.

By Harrow's side, Fast Eddie raised his rifle, aimed.

Harrow rested his hand on top of the barrel and exerted gentle downward pressure.

Fast Eddie resisted. "It's going to attack," he hissed.

"It's protecting its young," Harrow replied.

Behind the horned dinosaur, four speckled eggs lay clustered together in a nest of twigs and leaves – and bones.

Life and death went hand in hand in this lost world.

Fast Eddie lowered his rifle the rest of the way, made it safe, and said, "Understood, Lieutenant."

They slowly sidled out one by one, squeezing between the teeth.

Harrow was last out – and just in time to see Salgado Joe giving JJ a leg up. JJ grabbed the edge of a cavity in the bone and hauled and scrabbled his way onto the top of the skull.

Harrow was glad to see JJ seemed to have recovered fully from his traumatic experience the day before.

From the wide smile on his face as he stood atop the skull, JJ was more than recovered.

Harrow had seen this before during his army days. There was nothing like staring death in the face, and walking away, to give someone a love of life.

Sounding every bit as happy as he looked, JJ called out, "Come on up, boys, the view's fantastic."

His enthusiasm was infectious, and the others clambered gracelessly up onto the skull.

Harrow stood tall and looked out. A shiver went down his spine. For the first time he could almost see where the precipice reached the ground.

A leap of the imagination and he was almost there.

A hard march and he was.

Harrow smiled and allowed himself a moment to simply enjoy the sights of the lost world.

A sauropod lifting its head above the tops of the trees.

A majestic T-Rex moving into sight in the distance, slowly at first, then exploding into a sprint to chase its prey, a pack of clawed critters. Harrow knew who his money was on.

And at twelve 'o' clock there were a couple of dinosaurs of a type he'd never seen before trotting into view. Two new wonders.

To his uneducated eyes, they were elephant-sized rhinoceros that had been accessorized with three magnificent horns protruding from their skulls and a fan extending around their necks. The fan looked solid, like it could stop a bullet.

The pair of dinosaurs seemed peaceful enough, though, as they padded along.

There was a third one in view now. It was moving towards the pair – one of which was paying it no notice and walking on. The other stopped, turned to face the newcomer.

And charged.

It wasn't the quickest charge you'd ever seen. It was more like an amble with intent, but Harrow was sure that was what he was seeing.

And that the newcomer was charging back.

They closed on each other... collided. Their horns clashed with a sickening thud. They locked together. Both beasts twisted their necks, and dug their feet into the ground, grappling furiously.

One began to be forced backwards. It struggled on, but it was clear to Harrow it was fighting a losing battle now.

It pulled its head free and staggered away.

The victor turned and trotted over to the dinosaur which had been a spectator to the contest, and mounted it.

It was the oldest story in the world.

The winner gets the girl.

"It's the dinosaur Salgado Joe," Fast Eddie said with a cheeky grin on his face. "It's big, it's ugly, it scores!"

Harrow sighed. Wonderful moment well and truly over, he slid down off the skull.

He landed on the rocks – next to a long pair of antennas which were wriggling into view from under the tip of the jawbone.

In backyards in his old home town thousands of miles away, millipedes would be wriggling out of cracks between paving stones.

As the others landed heavily back down on the rocks around him, Harrow watched a millipede wriggling out into the open.

This one was nine feet long and a foot wide. A shell undulated on its back as its many legs moved, and what he'd first thought were antennas looked more like a duo of scorpion's stingers.

He shivered. His dislike of bugs was developing into a phobia.

He wasn't alone.

"Permission to use up a couple of bullets on it?" Fast Eddie asked.

Apart from those weird stinger antennas, Harrow did not think the millipede posed them any threat.

But...

Gross.

"Permission granted."

Fast Eddie aimed and let loose a couple of shots. Both struck the millipede's shell and went through.

The millipede stopped wriggling along for a moment, then started up again.

Fast Eddie swore. Shot it again.

This time the millipede did not even pause.

Half a dozen cracks in its shell showed where the bullets had pierced but it seemed to be oblivious.

"It's a damn zombie bug," one of the Banjo twins

said.

"You have to shoot it in the brain," his brother added.

JJ scratched his chin and asked, "What if it does not have a brain?"

Fast Eddie growled, "Let's find out."

He blasted the millipede's head with automatic fire.

It was utter overkill.

When he took his finger off the trigger, the millipede's head had been obliterated and it was lying on its back.

"Why are its legs still moving?" JJ asked.

A question no one wanted an answer to.

They moved off.

Hard miles followed. Harrow set the pace. He was getting tunnel vision now. The precipice loomed larger as they got ever closer.

As it did, the circle of life turned around them, sharp as a scythe in this lost world, leaving death, predators feeding on prey, cannibalism, and the sounds of either more slaughtering or breeding in its wake.

It was hard to tell. Hard to care with the prize increasingly in sight.

With dusk approaching, Harrow dropped his backpack.

He looked around. There was enough space around for the Pastor to set his traps, clear views to the undergrowth. The stream was near enough to collect water. Dozens of dragonflies were settled by its banks as well.

Perhaps they slept as well.

Like T-Rex.

Like he would the moment he could finally drag himself into his sleeping bag.

He turned back to the others, said, "We'll make camp for the night here."

CHAPTER 14

The first bug of the day.

Whatever had brushed his cheek was gone before he could waft it away.

Harrow yawned as he made one more circuit of the camp, another sentry shift almost done. Bodies were stirring nearby, sitting up still fully enveloped in their sleeping bags.

It was like a low-budget horror movie, especially when faces started to appear. It was the Dawn of the Bitten Dead.

A fart erupted inside Salgado Joe's sleeping bag, rousing anyone who was still sleeping.

JJ among them. He had a coughing fit then muttered hoarsely, "I thought the great outdoors was meant to be good for you."

Harrow laughed.

They'd made it through another night and today, Lady Luck willing, they'd reach the base of the precipice.

He rubbed his chin and noticed there was a wasp hovering in the air a few feet in front of him. It was three inches long with red and white stripes on its thorax. Not a friendly visitor.

But as long as it kept its distance...

He shouldered his rifle, leaving both hands free to swing the baseball bat in case it didn't.

Salgado Joe broke wind again.

Fast Eddie pulled a face at the toxic smell that drifted out of Salgado Joe's sleeping bag as he unzipped it.

The second wasp, crawling on the ground nearby, did not seem to mind.

Harrow watched its slow progress over the rocks then noticed yet another wasp hovering near the stream.

Another zipping past his face.

He wondered if they had inadvertently camped near a nest of the things in the undergrowth.

It did not matter now. The morning light was streaming down, and they'd be out of there soon enough.

He glanced around the borders of their camp one last time to check that nothing that stood upright to bite was loitering nearby.

He could not see anything to worry about.

The only other living things bigger than a fly in sight were the dozens of dragonflies he'd seen at dusk.

They hadn't stirred yet. Their gossamer wings – and some had spans pushing three feet – were still.

It was an unusual spectacle – but so much was in this strange place.

He told himself not to worry about it.

But he was. He had a growing feeling something was wrong.

He walked towards the nearest dragonflies. Saw

when he came close enough that one was little more than a husk and that its exoskeleton was split open.

And that the dragonflies around it were anything but still.

They were a riot of movement.

Inside.

Countless dark forms were shifting around beneath the dragonflies' exoskeletons. He stepped right up to one, peered down at it, and saw the exoskeleton split, the wasp's head appear.

It crawled out, its wings flickering.

Harrow took a step back and looked around at all the dragonflies, at the way they were all pulsing within, about to break apart.

He'd seen parasitical wasps in jungles before and knew how they laid their eggs in host insects or even spiders in some cases. The larva then consumed their hosts from the inside, until they were ready to leave and take flight.

That had been nothing, compared to this.

Harrow staggered away, not wanting to see, but unable to look away, as hundreds of wasps broke free of their hosts' remains.

He could hear the horrified cries of the others behind him. Without turning around, he said, "Do not make any sudden movements. They will only sting if they feel threatened."

"If they feel threatened...!" JJ spluttered.

Harrow wanted to abandon everything and run for the hills, but he had to keep a lid on that.

He said, "Pack what you can and let's move slowly out."

Someone had once told him that bravery was keeping the terror inside until you were safe and could let it out. A pressure cooker approach that was seriously flawed.

One Harrow would keep taking because he knew no other way.

"It's going to be fine," he said and started walking.

The wasps were swarming, darkening the sky every way Harrow looked. He realized with mounting dread that there was nothing else for it.

They would have to walk through the swarm.

He closed his mouth and his eyes to try and keep the wasps out, and once more put one foot in front of the other.

He could feel the bodies of wasps striking his face as he moved into the swarm. They were touching his hands, his neck.

Landing on him. Crawling into his clothes. Crawling through his scalp.

He was desperate to break into a run, but he knew if he did, they would begin to sting.

More wasps were descending onto him. His face was covered with them. A moving mask of wasps.

One foot in front of the other.

He had to keep going.

He had no idea where the others were. He was moving blind and all he could hear was the buzzing of thousands of wings.

All he could feel was wasps moving over him.

He wanted to scream. Only the wasps would crawl into his mouth, down his throat.

Deeper and deeper.

Until they finally began to sting.

He would die in agony, but that would not be the end of it.

The wasps would lay their eggs inside him. The eggs would become larva and begin to feed on his flesh.

The scavengers would not touch his corpse. They would know it was tainted, riddled with a multitude of larva.

The larva would grow, pupate, until they were ready to bite through his cold, dead skin and rise into the air.

A new swarm. Born from him.

Harrow felt a hand touch his shoulder.

He realized there were tears running down his face – and that was all. There was nothing else on his skin.

He opened his eyes.

JJ was standing in front of him.

"It's okay," JJ said. "We made it. We're clear of the wasps."

Harrow looked back and saw they'd left the dark mass of the swarm behind.

He walked on in silence, feeling ashamed and confused and scared by the way he had lost it.

He tried to focus back on the task at hand.

The precipice was looming larger and larger as they steadily neared its base.

Harrow shielded his eyes from the sunlight with his hand and glanced up. He could just about make out the river cascading over the top of the precipice that had carried the thieves to their deaths, and their haul with them, but the waterfall seemed to peter out miles above.

He looked down, blinked a bunch of times. As the imprint the dazzling glare had left on his vision lingered, he wondered how Max was doing up there.

If he was gazing down into the hidden depths at that very moment in time.

Or taking a piss over the edge.

Harrow managed a smile as this random mental image brought him out of his funk.

Harrow threw a casual salute Max's way, miles above, and said, "See you soon."

Harrow was feeling better. His skin was the same mass of old and new bites, his feet felt like two big blisters, and his torn and filthy clothes hung loose off his frame because of all the weight he'd lost.

The others were in the same state.

And from the determined expressions on their faces, none of them gave a damn.

Harrow, now out and out grinning, put one big blister in front of the other.

There was, at an educated guess, five miles to go.

Five miles was nothing.

CHAPTER 15

"You ever feel like there is a higher power controlling over lives... and sometimes they are just plain jerking us around?"

As he stared out over the water, Harrow had to agree with JJ.

The lake filled the gorge, blocking their way.

It must have been the source of the stream that had flowed steadily alongside them since they'd entered the gorge. And it was way too deep to wade through.

"We'll need to swim," Harrow said.

It was the only way, and they could do it. Their destination was achingly close. They could do it. They would do it.

"Er, Lieutenant."

"What is it Salgado?" Harrow asked. "Please don't tell me you can't swim."

The big man looked at his feet. Beneath all the bite marks it was close to impossible to tell, but Harrow could have sworn that Salgado Joe was blushing.

"Everyone can swim!" Harrow protested.

Salgado Joe shook his head, looking more ashamed by the moment.

"Jeez," JJ muttered.

Fast Eddie laughed and said, "Maybe we could

use Salgado Joe as a raft."

Harrow grinned at the prospect. And because Fast Eddie had given him an idea. He turned to look at the Banjo twins.

"We're on it," they said in unison.

"JJ and Pastor on escort duty. Fast Eddie and Salgado Joe, manual labor," Harrow ordered. The Banjo twins were already heading back to the jungle for the raw materials. The others scurried after them, leaving Harrow brooding and staring out over the water.

It was still. Too still.

He was tempted to call the Pastor back over and ask him to toss a couple of sticks of dynamite into the lake to flush out any creatures that might be lurking below the surface, but decided to leave it.

Better they try and make it across as quickly and quietly as they could. Leave the monsters slumbering in the depths.

Harrow shuddered as he watched a lone ripple spreading out over the surface of the water.

Over at the edges of the jungle he could hear wood being cut. Salgado Joe yelling out, "I got this." Fast Eddie yelping, "Watch my foot!"

An hour and a lot of shouting later, a raft sat by the side of the lake. It was skillfully constructed from tree trunks bound together by vines by the talented twins.

Harrow said, "Load her up, boys."

"Are we not going to name the raft first?" JJ

asked.

"How about Salgado's Shame?" Fast Eddie suggested.

Salgado Joe swung a slap at the top of Fast Eddie's head, but deliberately missed.

Harrow grinned and asked Salgado Joe, "Of all the many ladies you have loved, was there one who stood out above all the rest? I'm thinking, we can name the boat after her."

After a moment's deep thought, Salgado Joe answered, "Daisy. She was my first."

"Right," Harrow said. "I name this vessel Daisy. May she carry us safely over deep waters."

"Your first, and your favorite cousin as well," Fast Eddie chipped in.

The fist Salgado Joe made looked like it was headed for Fast Eddie's face. And there would be no swerving this time.

Before the punch could be thrown, Harrow bellowed, "Move your asses!"

The Banjo twins dragged the raft onto the water and took up positions at the front and rear with the paddles they'd also made. Backpacks were thrown onboard, boots hit the deck, and Fast Eddie heaved against the bank to push them off.

It was not a long journey. Harrow estimated twenty minutes or so. He could see the rocks rising from the water's edge on the far side, the undergrowth spreading out over dry ground.

Behind him, the Banjo twins were coordinating

their strokes. JJ and Fast Eddie were sitting cross-legged with their rifles draped over their laps. The Pastor was trimming the fuse on a stick of dynamite, and Salgado Joe was pacing up and down the deck of the raft nervously.

His bulk shifting this way and that was making the raft rock slightly.

It was not dangerous, but it was noticeable. Annoying.

"Sit down or at least stand still," Harrow told him impatiently.

"C... can't," Salgado Joe replied. "What if the raft capsizes? What if we fall in? The water's so deep."

Harrow had never seen the big man so uptight.

"None of that is going to happen," Harrow said. "Please, Salgado, give it a rest."

"C... can't."

"How come you never learned to swim anyway?" Fast Eddie asked.

"All the rivers near where I grew up were infested with alligators. Big bastards. They'd take a grown man easy, grab him in their jaws and spin him. They wouldn't kill by biting though. They'd drag their victim down and drown him then leave the corpse until the flesh rotted. They liked their meat rancid, you see, the local gators. And it was only when it was good and rotten, then they'd tear flesh from bone and feed. Big bastards," he said again, and shivered.

Fast Eddie looked as if he was considering this grisly fate for a moment, then he said, "Way you already smell, Salgado, I don't think the alligators round here would have too long to wait before they tucked in to their fetid feast."

Before Salgado Joe could respond, Harrow said, "Enough. Fast Eddie, stop baiting Salgado. Salgado, stay the hell still."

"Sorry, Lieutenant," Fast Eddie said, doing a very bad job of hiding a smirk as he did.

Salgado Joe did not respond.

He was staring out over the lake. His mouth hung open. Sweat dripped down his face.

"G... Gator," he said.

Harrow followed the big man's gaze. He saw a dark shape in the water.

It was not moving.

"It's a dang log," Fast Eddie said dismissively.

Harrow hoped that was the case. He could see more of the object now under the water. It was long. Hellishly long. With an uneven, ridged surface.

"Oh, shit."

Harrow heard his own voice say this as if it was coming from a distance.

He felt light headed. Sick. Could not think straight.

There was an alligator in the lake.

And it was a destroyer of reason.

The scale-clad behemoth rose higher in the water. It was side on to them. Its jaw alone was longer than the raft. The eye they could see radiated menace. Its fangs were still hidden beneath the surface, their promise of death unseen.

It began to turn, slow and deliberate, until it was facing them.

Harrow found his voice: "Combined fire. Aim at its head."

"That thing looks bulletproof, Lieutenant." Fast Eddie sounded beaten when he said this but was raising his rifle anyway.

"I know. I don't think we can kill it. But if we can keep it at bay until we get to the other side, we should be able to outrun it on land."

Death was not a done deal here. Harrow had to keep believing that.

"Dwayne, Grant, paddle like hell. You other men, on my command."

He gave them five seconds to aim.

"Fire!"

A volley of gunfire rang out.

He heard the cracks of multiple discharges, saw the water dance where the shots had missed. He could tell these were outliers. Their aim was mostly true.

They were striking their target with ferocious automatic fire.

And the alligator was turning away.

He could not make out any damage to its scales, but they were getting to it. Making it understand this prey was more trouble than it was worth. Must have been.

"Don't let up," he yelled over the sound of the gunfire.

He glanced at the Banjo twins. Veins were standing out on their temples as they strained to propel the raft through the water.

He glanced at the shore. A few more minutes and they could jump the last few feet, might not even have to run for their lives if the alligator was giving up.

He looked back at the beast. It was side on again, and still turning.

Then its vast tail rose out of the water... and whipped back down, crashing into the water, creating a wave that rushed towards them, and struck the raft.

The raft rocked violently, sending Fast Eddie sprawling.

The rest of them managed to keep their feet, but the alligator's tail was striking again, sending another wave rolling high through the water.

The collision threw one side of the raft into the air. Fast Eddie slid towards the edge. JJ tried to grab him, but missed Fast Eddie's outstretched hand and the pair of them toppled into the water.

Harrow watched them fall. He felt utterly helpless. The alligator was deliberately trying to overturn the raft and it was going to succeed.

A few more whips of that tail and they'd all be thrashing around in the water. Then the alligator could pick them off at will.

He turned to see a fresh wave ploughing through the water towards them. Just before it struck, the Pastor sent a stick of dynamite spinning through the air towards the alligator.

Harrow rode the bucking raft and saw the dynamite fall sickeningly short.

The Pastor had slipped over but was struggling back to his feet. He took out a new stick of dynamite and shouted over to Harrow, "I can't pitch this far enough. How's your swing?"

Harrow understood and planted his feet. A new wave was seconds away. The Pastor was lighting the fuse, throwing the dynamite Harrow's way.

There was no time to do anything other than swing the baseball bat at the dynamite.

It was a clean strike. The dynamite span through the air. It flew the length of the alligator and exploded inches from the monster's eyes.

Its whole body thrashed violently in the water, sending more waves their way.

But these were the last.

The alligator was moving away, sliding back beneath the surface until it was once again merely a dark presence.

And then it was gone. Returned to the depths.

Fast Eddie spluttered, "Out of the park."

CHAPTER 16

The Banjo twins made the spiked pole from a branch. Salgado Joe handed over what was left of his t-shirt for the flag.

JJ did the honors.

He planted the flagpole in a crevice between the rocks and said, "I claim this land and all finds made on it in the name of the assembled company of fine and upstanding men. From this day forth, all governments can go whistle and the IRS can kiss our hairy asses."

Everyone burst into applause. There were handshakes, a bear hug or two.

They had made it. They'd made camp in the shadow of the precipice, a fire was lit, coffee brewing. They'd set traps and eat later.

Standing there, Harrow felt the kind of pride he'd thought he'd never experience again after the army screwed him over.

Well, screw them now.

There was still work to do, though. Gold to be found.

He clapped his hands together, the nerves, the exhaustion slipping away as the excitement built inside him. He addressed the others, "While there's daylight left, we will make a start on the search for the coins. Let's work wise. We will divide the area into grids and do a meticulous fingertip search. Once each grid is complete, we'll mark it with a stack of stones and move on. Everyone clear on that?"

There were thumbs-ups and grins in response.

JJ said, "Damn right!"

Salgado Joe clenched his fists.

Fast Eddie said, "There's one thing I am not sure about, Lieutenant?"

"What's that?"

"Who the hell is that?"

Fast Eddie pointed at the man standing at the edge of the jungle.

He had a thick gray beard that reached down to his waist and long gray hair that stuck out in every direction. A pair of reading glasses were perched on the end of his nose and he wore the tattered remains of a three-piece suit that was caked with dirt. A red bowtie hung loose around the neck of a dirty shirt that had been white once, a long time ago.

Harrow's hand had automatically drifted to his rifle, but he left it slung over his shoulder.

This stranger, whoever he was, did not look like a threat.

In this lost world where dinosaurs still roamed, he looked like a cross between the missing link and an elderly librarian who had fallen on hard times.

And he looked scared.

Harrow put his shock to one side, made a small, calm gesture with his hand to tell everyone to lower guns that had been instinctively raised.

He put a friendly smile on his face, walked over nice and calm and easy to where the stranger was standing and said, "My name is Tom Harrow."

The stranger opened his mouth and looked like he was trying to speak.

It was clearly a struggle. He grimaced and coughed and finally managed to say, "It has been so long." His eyes started to brim with tears and he wiped a filthy sleeve across his nose. "So long."

Harrow held out his hand to shake.

The stranger stared at it with a mixture of confusion and awe on his face.

How long was so long? Harrow pondered this while he kept his hand stretched out. How long had it been since this bedraggled individual had seen another human being?

The stranger raised his right hand slowly. It shook badly, and kept shaking as he took Harrow's hand in his own.

"John Walker," he said, his already hoarse voice breaking with emotion. "Professor John Walker. It is very good to meet you, Mr. Harrow. You and your colleagues."

"Likewise," Harrow replied. "Though I have to tell you, Professor Walker, that we were really not expecting to meet anyone else here."

"Tell me about it," Walker said and smiled with his eyes.

Their hands were still clasped. Harrow put his

other hand on Walker's shoulder. He could feel the old man's bones through the filthy fabric and noticed how his clothes hung off his frame. He did not look emaciated, though. He seemed more wiry, and there was strength in his handshake as the shakes diminished.

"The coffee should be almost brewed by now. Would you care to join us?" Harrow asked, the search pushed to the back of his mind for now. "We don't have cream or sugar but the coffee is good and strong."

Walker laughed. "My diary is free. So, yes, I'd be delighted to join you, Mr. Harrow."

With an arm draped over Walker's bony shoulder, Harrow led him back over to the camp and introduced him to the gang.

They were more polite than he'd ever seen them. Walker was soon handed a coffee. Salgado Joe rolled a boulder over for the newcomer to use as a seat.

With Walker settled, Harrow could not hold himself back.

"So," he asked. "What brought you here?"

Walker sipped the coffee, and looked wistful as he said, "I used to teach at a faculty in a Southern city. It was not the most prestigious establishment but I loved my work. The students were keen to learn and I did my best to share my passion for anthropology with them. I would say that was my chosen subject, but it actually felt like the subject had chosen me. You see, I was gripped from an early age by society – by what binds us and divides us, what drives us on and what holds us back. More and more as my own studies advanced, I was drawn to study ancient cultures. The past often holds the key to the future, in my humble opinion."

He took another sip of his coffee before continuing. "I taught at the university for a decade and the department was flourishing alongside the young people who studied there, but then there were… allegations."

His hands began to shake again and hot coffee sloshed out of the beaker and landed on his leg. If he felt it burn, he did not show it as he went on.

"I was accused of plagiarizing the work of other academics in my articles in journals and of defrauding the department of fees that had been provided by benefactors. These were lies. All filthy lies. But they would not go away. The academic world can be a small, bitter place. Ambition overreaches talent. Grudges fester. I was, it became increasingly clear, the victim of a vendetta. I wanted to stay and fight but the university gave me no option. I was suspended without pay and I could not afford a lawyer to fight them, so one morning I packed up my bags and left. I drifted from place to place and eventually crossed the border. It was in a small town, thousands of miles away from the back stabbing world of academia, that I discovered a way to restore my reputation and give an irrefutable two fingers to those who had caused my downfall. I heard tales of an ancient precipice which was the site for human sacrifices. These took place long before the Europeans came and brought their gods and diseases. The priests of this land were offering villagers to the old gods that they believed dwelled at the base of the precipice. They were cutting the villagers' throats and hurling them into the depths. I was fascinated. All I needed to do was find proof of these acts and present my findings, so I used the last of my meagre savings to hire local guides and travelled down into the gorge which leads here. I discovered so much more than evidence of a dead religion. I found an abundance of life that all humankind thought lost forever. Over the years that have followed I have devoted myself to a study of the gorge. My guides were all killed or succumbed to diseases but I persevered. For so long. Too long perhaps. Because I do not know now if I can ever go back. I am old and tired and I think the journey would kill me. I..."

His voice, which had grown weaker and weaker as he had spoken, finally trailed away and he stared morosely into the fire.

Harrow could not leave the old man to wallow.

There was another question he had to answer.

One that mattered more than anything else in the whole damn world at that moment in time.

Harrow glanced at JJ, and could see he was thinking the same thing.

They all were.

Harrow asked, "In your time here, have you come across gold coins? They would be scattered across the ground, somewhere within a wide radius of here. Could maybe have still been in saddlebags."

Walker looked up from the fire. He seemed puzzled by the question.

Harrow felt his heart sink.

If Walker had not stumbled across any gold coins in all his years in the gorge, then the odds of Harrow and the others finding their fortune and turning their misbegotten lives around would spiral towards zero.

And they had come so far. Given so much.

Walker drained the last of his coffee, and shook his head. Said quietly, "No."

Harrow felt like he had been stabbed in the heart.

"I am sorry, Mr. Harrow, but I have not seen anything like that in all my time here. Is... is that what brought you to the base of the precipice? The prospect of gold?"

It was a reasonable question, and Harrow should have given a straight answer.

But he could not speak.

All his hopes and dreams were crashing around him. He put his head in his hands. He heard Salgado Joe say, "Bastard idiot!"

He could have been talking about himself. Could have been talking about any of them.

They had been so caught up in the adventure, so dazzled by the thoughts of lost gold, that they had gone on a fool's errand.

For this.

A bug sat on the back of Harrow's hand, feeding on him. Harrow could see its revolting body bloating as it sucked his blood.

He did not even have the strength to swat it.

He was aware that Walker was still looking at him, waiting for an answer.

"It was." Harrow dredged the words up. "We met someone. A thief. An old man now. He told us how long ago the gang he ran with stole a fortune. They died trying to escape with it. Fell, gold and all, off the top of the precipice. And years later, along we came. And we followed the trail. We might just as well have jumped over the edge ourselves, saved ourselves a world of trouble."

He tried to smile. Tried to show he was not beaten.

And failed.

Because that's what losers did.

Most people would have looked away by now but Walker's gaze held. He looked Harrow in the eye and said, "I am truly sorry to hear that. I am sorry that I seem to have been the one to dash your dreams. And I know that turning to drink solves nothing in the long term, but perhaps a shot of strong liquor would help ease your pain a little."

He reached into a pocket in his disheveled suit

jacket and produced a silver hip flask. "When I set off on my journey, this flask held a very fine brandy. That didn't last long I'm afraid to say. But my time here has not been devoted entirely to study. I have become rather a good brewer of wine. Would you care to sample some?"

He unscrewed the cap of the hip flask and held it out to Harrow.

Who did not hesitate. He accepted the hip flask and took a long drink.

He lowered the hip flask and the booze hit him. Hard. It was like one of the Pastor's sticks of dynamite had gone off in his head.

His mouth was on fire, his mind reeling. He gasped and swayed on his rocky perch. He wiped his watering eyes and managed to say, "What the hell is this made from?"

Walker grinned, looking more like a mischievous urchin than an aged academic. "Fruits that have fallen from their trees that have then fermented for years, plus one or two special ingredients. I have been experimenting over the years and I am proud of this particular vintage."

Harrow shook his head to try and clear it. "As wine goes, it kicks!"

Walker laughed. Salgado Joe reached out. "Give me some of that, Lieutenant. Boy, do I need a drink."

Harrow found himself laughing as he watched Salgado Joe taking a long gulp of the wine. JJ, Fast

Eddie, the Banjo twins, even the Pastor did the same.

The Pastor shivered as the wine went down then exclaimed, "Blessed be the booze!"

That set Harrow off even more. He was laughing fit to burst. Holding his guts. His eyes were streaming. The world was spinning... and blurring... and disappearing.

CHAPTER 17

Harrow opened his eyes and groaned. His head was pounding and his guts ached.

He tried to sit up, which made everything feel worse. He was convinced he was going to be violently sick. He'd had plenty of hangovers in his time, but this was worse.

He took a series of slow, deep breaths, and waited for the nausea to pass. When he felt confident that he was not going to empty the contents of his stomach at speed, he had another go at sitting up.

He made it, but was not sure it had been a good idea. He was dripping with sweat. Pain pulsed inside him. Even his eyeballs ached.

The brain cells that had not been killed roused themselves and he remembered what had got him into the state: Professor Walker, the hip flask, the wine.

It must have been stronger than any hick moonshine to have left him feeling like this.

He massaged his aching eyes and tried to bring the blurry shapes around him into focus.

It seemed he was not the only one who had been wiped out.

Salgado Joe was standing, though from the way he was swaying he looked like he had done twelve rounds in the ring with a heavyweight champion and his second had forgot to bring a towel.

JJ, the Pastor and Fast Eddie were all still sprawled out. One of the Banjo twins was pushing himself to his feet and looking around groggily.

"Grant," he said. "Where's Grant?"

Harrow gritted his teeth and stood up.

"Grant!" Dwayne yelled.

"He's probably gone to find somewhere private to throw up," Harrow said.

"No! He would not just walk off and leave me like that." Dwayne sounded like he was losing it, but Harrow did not question him.

The bond between the twins ran deep.

"We'll find him," Harrow said. "He'll be okay, you both will."

Dwayne did not look like he believed a word of that.

Harrow did not blame him. There was something clearly very wrong here.

His addled mind was catching up to the fact that it wasn't just one of the Banjo twins that was missing. There was no sign of Walker either.

The sickening thought that dinosaurs might have taken both of them struck Harrow. More than might. That was the likeliest explanation.

But there was a chance it was something else, that they were both still alive.

And while there was a chance, no matter how slim…

"Salgado," Harrow shouted at the big man. "Get the others up and moving then follow me and Dwayne." He faced the distraught twin and said, "Let's go find your brother and the Professor."

Harrow automatically grabbed his baseball bat, and the two of them hurried away from the camp. The light was fading as dusk approached but it was still light enough for him to see their surroundings clearly.

There was no sign of Grant or Walker in the open which meant they must be somewhere in the jungle.

But where to begin?

Dwayne was not slowing to think, he was rushing on in.

Harrow followed hot on his heels, not knowing what else to do.

They were running blind. Could have been running in completely the wrong direction.

He just did not know.

Then he saw... he thought he saw, a trail ahead. The ground had been disturbed.

As if something had been dragged along it.

A fresh corpse, or two. Or prey still struggling with the last of its strength.

He pushed these hideous thoughts aside. Ran on.

He saw the trail veer to their right. Throwing a dice, he followed it. He did not tell Dwayne why he was running this way. And he did not want Dwayne to ask.

One of those corpses might have been his twin

brother. The prey, his closest kin.

Harrow kept running.

Kept hoping.

Until suddenly they were in the open.

Harrow stopped dead. Dwayne did the same.

They were standing at the edge of a clearing.

Staring at an aberration.

Bones were piled on the ground ahead of them. Skulls and ribcages, femurs, tibias, tails and teeth all mixed chaotically together. The skeletal remains of dinosaurs and human beings.

Through the gaps in the bones Harrow could see hundreds of gold coins glinting in the evening light.

They had found the lost treasure.

And it did not matter – because Grant was lying on top of the vile construct of bone and coins. His wrists and ankles were bound with vine. His mouth gagged.

Standing next to him was Walker.

He no longer looked like a tired old man. He seemed reinvigorated. He had a gleam in his eyes and a dark, disturbing smile.

And he had seen Harrow and Dwayne.

"Welcome," he cried out in a manic voice. "Welcome to the ceremony, one and all. Here at this altar I have constructed to the old gods. I, their last true servant."

It was clear to Harrow that the academic was gone – replaced by a fanatic. A madman, who raved on.

"It has been a thousand years and more since homage was paid to the old gods. Since we pathetic mortals paid our dues. Well, the time has come for blood to be spilled. I sacrifice this man to you, my terrible lizards, my beautiful lords."

He took a knife out of his belt.

Realizing with a jolt of horror what was about to happen, Harrow launched himself forwards.

"Grant!" Dwayne screamed.

Harrow was at the base of the bones.

The tip of the knife hung over Grant's chest. Walker's hands were steady now as they held it.

Steady, determined.

Harrow scrambled up bones that cracked and shifted under his feet, but he had the momentum. He kept ascending, swung his baseball bat, was about to knock the knife from Walker's grip.

But the knife was flashing down.

Entering Grant's chest.

It was in up to the hilt.

Harrow swung higher. The bat connected with Walker's skull. His eyes fell back in his head and he toppled away.

Dealt with.

But too damn late.

Dwayne was by his brother's side. His hands were on Grant's chest, on either side of the blade. Blood was running over his fingers and he was looking deep into Grant's eyes and saying, "It's going to okay. It's going to be okay."

Grant was looking back up at his brother, and Harrow could see the love in his eyes.

And then there was nothing in his gaze.

Grant was gone.

Dwayne lowered his head and sobbed.

Harrow moved over to Dwayne, put a hand gently on his shoulder and said in a quiet voice, "Come on, let's get your brother out of here."

Dwayne's face was streaked with tears and he looked very young and lost.

He nodded, then used his knife to remove the gag and cut the vines wrapped around Grant's ankles and wrists.

Harrow heard footsteps, saw the others had made it.

They looked devastated at the sight of Dwyane tending to his dead brother, though they could not have had any idea of what had happened here.

Harrow would explain later.

"Give us a hand," he said to them, and they moved forwards as one and helped Dwayne lift Grant's body off the foul altar.

Harrow stepped down onto the ground – and felt the first tremor.

He knew what it was. Saw from the glances exchanged between them that the others did as well.

All apart from Dwayne who was lost in his grieving.

The ground shook again. There was the sound of branches breaking, and the dinosaur charged into the clearing.

The T-Rex towered over them. Its jaws opened. It roared at them with savage fury.

Even though he was terrified, Harrow was in awe of its power, its primal majesty.

This old god.

He looked the dinosaur in the eye. He felt no malice towards it.

This was its kingdom and he was an intruder and he was going to pay the price for that with his life.

"My lord!"

Harrow span round. Walker was back on his feet. Blood coated his face from the head wound Harrow had inflicted with the baseball bat.

"My lord!" Walker cried out again. He started to stagger towards the T-Rex and raised his arms as if in praise. "I have brought you these sacrifices in homage to your…"

He did not finish. The T-Rex leant over and closed its jaws around him.

It raised its head back up. Walker was caught in its grip. His screams were muffled. His legs kicked out.

The T-Rex bit down.

Half of Walker fell to the ground. His body had been severed at the waist. What was left of him lay there. His legs kicked out grotesquely one more time.

Above them, the T-Rex was devouring the chunk of prey. More fresh meat waited below.

Harrow knew this was their chance to escape.

He pointed frantically towards the path which had brought them there, and the others understood.

They moved quickly, carrying Grant's body with them, and within minutes were back at the camp.

They put Grant on the ground and formed a protective circle around him and waited.

But there was no sign of the T-Rex.

The prey it had eaten must have satisfied its hunger for now.

That was all Harrow could think.

They remained standing in their circle though. There was no sign of the T-Rex but there were dark shapes circling above.

They had smelt blood. Smelt death.

Salgado Joe, JJ and Fast Eddie had rifles raised, ready to shoot them out of the sky the moment they swooped.

Harrow turned to Dwayne and said, "We won't let anything go near your brother. We will find a safe place to bury him in the morning."

Dwayne shook his head. "There isn't a grave we can dig that will be deep enough here." He looked at his brother then said, "Build up the fire."

It was the Pastor who broke away from the circle and gathered up more kindling and added them to the fire.

As its flames rose into the sky, they carried Grant's body over and laid it tenderly onto the fire.

The body did not burn easy. It was a hideous

thing to witness, but Dwayne did not look away, so none of them did.

They stood and watched and added more wood as it was needed until all there was left was ashes drifting away into the night.

Dwayne finally stepped back from the pyre. He said in a quiet, steady voice, "I am still going to open the workshop. And both of our names will be over the door. I will never forget you, my brother."

He wiped away a fresh tear. "Now, let's go claim our gold."

CHAPTER 18

Running out of ammunition a few days into the journey back along the gorge was a bitter blow, but one they'd known was coming. The Pastor meanwhile was down to his last stick of dynamite. He wore it around his neck on a looped length of vine and clutched it now and then to mutter a prayer.

The rest of them took comfort in knowing that, thanks to the gold coins carried in their backpacks, they were rich.

Lying in a den dug in a huge pile of manure to hide from a passing dinosaur was made bearable by the thoughts of the good times that were coming up. Five-star hotel suites, champagne, stretch-limos.

Picture them until the ground stops shaking and then shake off the dung beetles and the spiders and spit out the shit then get moving again.

Slice a snake's belly open with a knife before it could drive its fangs in and imagine its blood was a fine, expensive wine, its raw rubbery meat a rib eye steak grilled to perfection.

This was how they survived.

Harrow, JJ, Fast Eddie, Salgado Joe, the Pastor and Dwayne Banjo scrambled up the last few feet and found themselves standing on level ground, the gorge far below them, a lost world once more undisturbed by man.

Another few hours and they would be back to the jeeps and Max, and from there they were going to head to the first bar where they could buy ice-cold beer.

And where one lucky bar owner would find himself paid for a round with a gold coin and told to keep the change.

Harrow's feet ached as he trudged on. He'd become a collection of different pains – some stabbing, some aching, some constricted, some flaring – all contained within a wasted-away frame. Teeth had fallen out. Fingernails had fallen off, to be replaced by black, furry fungal infection.

He started whistling because none of those things mattered.

They were alive. They were wealthy.

And they had arrived. The jeeps were where they had left them. Max was leaning against the bonnet of one.

The old man looked good.

Though anything over and above a cadaver would in comparison.

Harrow grinned to himself at this thought. He waved at Max and called out, "We made it."

JJ, Fast Eddie and Salgado Joe raised their fists in triumphant salutes. Dwayne smiled but was more subdued. The Pastor was clutching his dynamite pendant and giving quiet thanks.

Max raised an arm – but did not wave back. He

gave a signal that Harrow did not understand.

Until a dozen men stepped out into the open. They were all heavily armed and had their weapons raised.

Harrow felt sick to the core.

He and his comrades, his friends... they had been betrayed.

Max was sidling forwards. "These fellows will relieve you of your backpacks," he said.

Four of the men holstered their guns and moved forwards.

Harrow exchanged glances with the others. He could tell they wanted to fight. But their ambushers were being careful to keep the line of fire clear.

The first hint of resistance and Harrow had no doubt he and the others would be mown down and the gold taken anyway.

He looked each of them in the eye, shook his head.

No.

They stood there with fury written on their faces as their backpacks were taken and carried back over to Max, who opened each one in turn and saw the coins.

"Well, I'm mightily grateful, I am. You going to all that trouble and, from the looks of you, risking life and limb, to retrieve my gold – you dumb sons of bitches, you Yankee scum!"

He patted one of the rucksacks and said to his armed thugs, "Load them up, boys. Like I promised you when I drove into your village, you're all going to get the payday of your lives."

He turned back to Harrow and the others. "As for you, to show you my gratitude, I won't have you killed. And you never know, you might even make it back to civilization alive."

With a last leer, he climbed into the nearest jeep.

It was one of four ramshackle vehicles parked up, Harrow could see now, and they were all gunning their engines into life and pulling away.

Taking the gold with them.

The feelings of sickness and the constant pain leeched out of him. Harrow was numb.

He'd been stitched up by the general, stitched up by Max. He had been bitten, attacked, almost eaten countless times.

But he was not beaten.

He reached into his pocket and took out the six gold coins he had put aside to give Max as his share.

Before he had learnt Max was the scum of the earth.

He held out the coins to the others and said, "You all take one. Dwanye, you have two. And I'll counsel no arguments on that matter."

"I am not going to argue with you, Lieutenant," Dwayne replied. "I'm just not going to take either of the coins. I say we keep them as one pot."

"Pool our resources," JJ said.

"Agreed," Fast Eddie added.

"This is the righteous path," the Pastor pronounced.

Salgado Joe nodded then said, "We can pay for a ride to the plane and get back to the States."

"We can pay for digs and new clothes," Fast Eddie threw in.

"And plan our next mission," JJ said.

Harrow looked at their ravaged, exhausted faces and smiled.

These dogs of war were not done yet.

End

Check out other great

Dinosaur Thrillers!

Gustavo Bondoni

TEST SITE HORROR

Lieutenant Max Alexeyev is a Russian Special Forces soldier. His job is to protect his country's interests at home and abroad, not to rescue overly ambitious reporters who have bitten off stories too big to chew. But when his unit gets called to a press event at a laboratory that has been invaded by dinosaurs, that's exactly what he finds himself doing. Fighting both prehistoric nightmares and the products of modern genetic experiments in the forests of the Ural Mountains, he battles for his own survival as well as that of alluring journalist Marianne Caruso and her peers.Unbeknownst to him, however, shadowy human forces are at work to ensure that no one spills the secrets of the research being done in the area.Will they live to tell the story of the Test Site Horror?

John Lee Schneider

AGE OF MONSTERS

Once upon a time, Dinosaurs ruled the Earth.But the Mesozoic era – the Age of Reptiles – came to its cataclysmic end sixty-five million years ago.The Age of Monsters begins tonight.And the world of humankind will crumble. Some will call it Judgment. Some will attempt to fight. Others will simply run. Most will just try and survive. But no one will escape.In the mountains. In the oceans. In the cities and towns. Even up in space.Where were YOU when the world ended?

 SEVERED**PRESS**

Check out other great

Dinosaur Thrillers!

Greig Beck

PRIMORDIA: IN SEARCH OF THE LOST WORLD

Ben Cartwright, former soldier, home to mourn the loss of his father stumbles upon cryptic letters from the past between the author, Arthur Conan Doyle and his great, great grandfather who vanished while exploring the Amazon jungle in 1908. Amazingly, these letters lead Ben to believe that his ancestor's expedition was the basis for Doyle's fantastical tale of a lost world inhabited by long extinct creatures. As Ben digs some more he finds clues to the whereabouts of a lost notebook that might contain a map to a place that is home to creatures that would rewrite everything known about history, biology and evolution. But other parties now know about the notebook, and will do anything to obtain it. For Ben and his friends, it becomes a race against time and against ruthless rivals. In the remotest corners of Venezuela, along winding river trails known only to lost tribes, and through near impenetrable jungle, Ben and his novice team find a forbidden place more terrifying and dangerous than anything they could ever have imagined.

William Meikle

THE LOST VALLEY

A remote high valley in the Canadian Rockies hides an ecosystem that has been lost in time. A small team of prospectors and their local guides are looking for gold. What they find is blood and terror and death. The valley's monstrous inhabitants are not about to let go of its secrets lightly.

Check out other great

Dinosaur Thrillers!

Doug Goodman

HUNTING WITH DINOSAURS

A hunting party is sent to catch and kill raptors that have escaped Dinosaur Falls Restricted Area and murdered nearby hikers. But the hunters find the raptors are unlike any creature they've ever hunted, and soon one lone bowhunter is running for his life through the Perdidos Mountains. He discovers an old wilderness survival trench and burrows in deep, but eventually the raptors come for him. His only salvation is to befriend a wolf hellbent on destroying the raptors. If they can come together, they can form a pack the world has never seen, but if they fail, the raptors are waiting with their sharp teeth and elongated claws...

Edward J. McFadden III

DINOSAUR RED

There's a doorway on Mars that has mankind's greatest minds perplexed. Deep beneath Aeolis Mons an ancient secret is revealed, and a team of explorers led by Forest Judge, Deputy Commander of Gale Base Alpha, are dispatched to investigate. The prehistoric gateway reveals a biosphere preserving Earth's distant past, and as Judge and crew stand on the threshold of mankind's greatest discovery the Martian ground trembles. A roar thunders from within, the doorway closes, and the team is trapped. Six mission specialists, each with unique skills, each with different reasons for wanting to break free of the primordial trap. To get home Judge is forced to choose between escape and changing the course of humanity. What will he do?